Forgotten Echoes

Once Upon a Midlife Series

Forgotten Echoes

Once Upon a Midlife Series

FL Journey

ISBN: 978-1-965176-15-3
EBOOK ISBN: 978-1-965176-16-0

Printed in the United States of America

Table of Contents

Chapter One

Gazing up at the building now in Alice's name, she couldn't believe it. It had always been a dream of Alice and her husband, Nathan, to own an antiques business so they could make money from their passion of going to thrift stores and estate sales. There had never been enough money or time to open a business.

Now Alice was looking up at the building in St. Augustine, Florida. In her hands was the deed naming the building at 10 Aviles Street as hers.

Next door to the right, as she faced the buildings, was a two-story white stone building. The large windows in front were covered, and the sign said, "Old Stone Architectural Preservation".

I bet it's owned by some old guy in a cable-knit sweater with leather elbow patches.

Alice approached the front of her new building.

She thought she saw the curtain move as if someone looked out the window, but it wasn't possible.

There must be a draft in the building.

She now owned the two-story, light brown stone building with similar large windows. But unlike the building next door, the front door was recessed, allowing for more window space. The windows were covered with sheets.

Yup. Those gotta go.

Looking at the stained sheets and dirty windows, Alice shuddered.

Moving to St. Augustine hadn't been in Alice's plans. In fact, lying around watching TV and eating ice cream had been her plans for the foreseeable future until her daughter, Tara, called to tell her she'd seen this cute antiques store for sale in St. Augustine.

Initially, she brushed her off, but then Alice got an email about a store for sale from a company she didn't remember subscribing to.

Tara was enlisted in the Navy and stationed in Jacksonville, Florida for the next three years, so Alice called and asked if she would go look at the place.

The following weekend, Tara drove down and called Alice on video chat to show her the building. The moment Tara entered the main room with all the antiques, Alice knew she would buy it if the price was right. Unfortunately, Tara couldn't go upstairs because they were remodeling, according to the realtor.

She called her financial advisor and let him know what was going on and to ask her lawyer to reach out. Alice assumed it would to be out of her price range, considering it was a prime location in downtown St. Augustine. Still, she had her lawyer look into it. It's why she kept her on retainer.

A few days later during their weekly call, Tara had asked if Alice had purchased the building because there was a 'Pending Sale' sign on the building.

"I haven't heard anything from Francis. He would've called me if he'd put money down on it. I haven't heard from Darla either, so I assume someone else offered more, or something was wrong with the building." Alice sighed as she put another scoop of ice cream into her bowl.

"You should probably have a cup of tea instead of ice cream, Mom." Tara heard the freezer door close.

"I do before bed; this is my before tea, before bed ice cream."

"Mom, ice cream isn't good for you." Tara was Alice and Nathan's only child, and she was always mature for her age, even though she was now an adult.

"Doctor said I'm great. If she isn't worried about it, you don't need to be."

"Maybe I should talk to the doctor, Mom, because I'm not sure you're telling her the whole truth."

"How about you go back to whatever you are doing, and I'll talk to you later?"

"Fine, but you'd better have a life insurance policy." Tara laughed as she hung up.

Smart ass.

Alice stared at her melted ice cream, now just a creamy puddle, and placed the bowl into the sink. She made her cup of tea and carried her laptop with her to her room.

Drinking her tea, she saw an email from Francis but decided it could wait until the morning. That night, she dreamed of Nathan. It wasn't uncommon for him to come to her in her dreams.

Love, buy the property. Leave this house, he told Alice.

But this is our home.

And? I'm dead. You need to live and stop with the chocolate mint ice cream. It makes the entire house smell like mint.

You're dead. Stop worrying about me enjoying my mint ice cream.

It had been a running joke between them for the twenty years they were together. Nathan hated mint, while Alice loved anything and everything mint. Before he died, he would say he could smell her mint ice cream throughout the entire house when she'd eaten it.

Yeah, but I can smell it. He faded from her dream.

Please don't go. I miss you.

Love, I'm always here with you.

Alice rolled her eyes in her dream.

Love you. Alice muttered as he completely faded away.

Lying in bed, she remembered the dream vividly, better than other times. She knew she was going to buy the property if the terms were good.

She sat at the kitchen table drinking her tea and opening her email. After looking over the email, she called Francis.

"Good morning, Ms. Alice. How are you today?" Francis' cheerful voice came over the line.

"I'm good. I saw your email last night and think we should go with it. Assuming, of course, the inspection and such come back with no major issues."

"Funny you should mention the inspection. This morning when I got to work, the owner's estate had sent a completed inspection. I called the inspector to make sure it was legitimate, and they said it was done recently."

"Strange. I've never heard of the seller preempting the inspection, and I've bought a fair number of houses," Alice commented.

"I agree, but I think they're very motivated. They even said in the email today that if we can close within a week, they'll drop 50,000 off their price and cover the inspection."

"Can we close quickly? Wait, they only want 300,000 for the place *and* the inventory? Sounds suspicious." Alice was shocked by the price.

"300,000 is low and closing quickly could be tough. I think it's worth it, though, if you really want to do it. I know you and Nathan had talked about opening an antique business. It's crazy, but you should do it."

Alice considered it and agreed. "You know what? Let's do it."

"I'll contact the bank and have them draft a wire transfer, since I'm guessing you don't want a loan?"

"No, I want to buy it outright." Alice had weighed her options. If something happened and the store didn't make money, she didn't want to owe a bank.

"Great. I'll call Darla and Teddy to get your house on the market." Francis had been their financial advisor for almost a decade. After Nathan died, he had done almost everything for Alice. "Do you want me to call a moving company?"

"Didn't the documents say it was fully furnished?"

"Yes, it is."

"Then no, I'll take the car and whatever I can fit inside it."

"Alice, are you sure? You have a big house."

"I'll take anything that has meaning to me. If I don't have enough room, I can always rent a storage unit and have it shipped or come back to get it. I don't need the furniture. Also, how much winter clothing will I need in Florida?" Alice glanced around her kitchen before continuing, "I have a lot I don't need, and it's just material items, anyway."

Francis laughed. "Alice, you're buying a business specializing in people wanting material goods."

"Not the same thing, and you know it." Alice laughed.

"True. With you moving, do you want me to find someone in Florida to take over for me?"

"No, I want you to get certified in Florida."

"Thank you. I have a nationwide certification, so I'm yours for as long as you'll have me."

"You didn't lead with that?" Alice and Francis laughed. "I guess I'll start looking at what I'm going to take, and you can start with whatever you do."

"Speak to you soon." Francis hung up.

Chapter Two

Moving to St. Augustine took less time than Alice expected it would since Tara had flown up to help her move. Driving 10 hours each day, it only took five days.

"Do you want to go with me to the signing?" Alice asked her daughter.

"No, I need to get back to the base tonight."

"Do you need to borrow the car? I can probably pick up a rental."

"No, I'm going to ride back to base with a friend who's here for the weekend."

"I'm sure it was just perfect timing, right?" Alice looked sideways at Tara.

"I have no clue what you mean." Tara smiled as Alice listened to her GPS instruct her on how to get to the hotel.

"Can I drop you off at the hotel and have you check in, so I can get this done before they close for the day?" Alice checked her watch and realized it was still on Oregon time. Calculating what time it was in Florida, she only had about 30 minutes to get there.

"Will do. I messaged Ty, and he should be leaving in about an hour. Do you want me to call you when I get to base?"

"Yes, please." Alice drove to the hotel. As she pulled in, she got out of the car and went around the car to hug Tara. "Love you."

Tara stretched before hugging her back. "Love you, Mom. If you need anything, call me."

Alice watched as Tara went into the hotel lobby before leaving to go to the escrow office for the keys and final paperwork.

***

When Alice opened the door, the secretary stood. "Hello, how can I help you?"

"I'm here to sign paperwork for 10 Aviles Street."

The secretary looked at her computer. "You must be Alice Tidway. Can I take a quick peek at your ID? I'll need to make a copy for the file."

"Of course. Here you go." Alice pulled her wallet from her purse and handed over her driver's license.

After making the copy, she handed the ID back. "Thank you. Ms. Smalls is ready for you."

"Thanks." Alice followed the secretary to a small conference room.

"Please have a seat, and she'll be with you soon."

Alice didn't sit right away. Instead, she wandered around admiring the black and white photos of St. Augustine. One building in the photos looked like the one she was buying. As she got closer to the photo, she heard someone clear their throat behind her.

Turning, she saw a small woman who was barely five feet tall. "Mrs. Tidway?" Her high-pitched voice was like nails on a chalkboard.

"Yes."

"Hi, I'm Ms. Smalls. I'll be completing the paperwork and giving you the keys. Do you need a map of the town?"

Ms. Smalls hopped onto the chair, and Alice could see out of the corner of her eye the woman's feet dangling like a child's.

Alice coughed to cover her laugh at the irony of the woman's name being Ms. Smalls and her being short enough for her feet to dangle as they were.

"Are you alright, Mrs. Tidway?" Ms. Smalls cocked an eyebrow at Alice.

"Yes, I apologize. I must have picked up a cough somewhere between Oregon and Florida. Probably too many days on the road."

"I'm sorry to hear." She moved the paperwork over to Alice.

"I need you to sign here and here." She pointed at two places on the same page.

Alice signed it and handed the paperwork and pen back to her.

Putting the pen down, Ms. Smalls looked over the page before pulling the keys out of her pocket and sliding them across the table.

"Here are your keys. I'll have Christina give you the purchase packet, including the deed, as you leave. Thanks for doing business with us."

Alice thanked her before following Ms. Smalls to the front of the office.

"Christina, can you please give Mrs. Tidway the property's closing packet? She already has the keys."

"Of course, Ms. Smalls."

Her left eye twitched before she turned to the filing cabinet behind her and pulled out a packet of papers. "Here you go. This is your copy to keep. If you need anything or lose your copy, we have a full backup copy here."

"Thank you, Christina." Alice took the packet from her.

"It's actually Cynthia, but you're welcome." She smiled.

"I am *so* sorry," Alice whispered.

"I've been here four years. It's fantastic." She rolled her eyes.

Alice snorted. "Sorry. I don't mean to laugh."

"My husband thinks it's the most hilarious thing in the world. It's alright." She motioned her hand as if she mimicking talking.

"If we see each other again, I promise to remember your name." Alice winked before turning to the door.

"Ms. Tidway?" Cynthia called out right before Alice reached the door.

"Yes?"

"I'm not supposed to tell people anything bad about their properties, but 10 Aviles Street? Allegedly, it's haunted." Cynthia looked serious, so Alice didn't laugh this time.

"Isn't everything in St. Augustine?" Alice replied.

"Yes, but this one's rumored to be *really* bad, but you didn't hear it from me."

"Thank you for the warning. I'll be careful." Alice didn't believe in ghosts and wasn't worried about the stories people told to scare their friends.

Back at the hotel, Alice slept but didn't dream aside from the words 'Forgotten Echoes' over and over.

***

She wrote the words down the following morning but didn't think much of them.

Chapter Three

Now or never

Alice drove and parked as close as she could to her new property. Finding parking in St. Augustine wasn't easy, so she was thankful she'd found a parking spot less than a quarter mile from the building.

Alice didn't see anyone particularly interested in her actions as she approached the glass door. Unlocking the door, she opened it, and a gust of stale air rushed out.

How can that be? They had plenty of people looking at this place, and I swore the sheet moved yesterday.

Alice entered the store and locked the door behind her, searching for the light switch at the same time.

Must be in the back.

She used the flashlight on her cell phone to guide her way through the clutter. Everywhere she looked, there was something. She wasn't paying attention and almost ran into the display case with a cash register on top of it. Shaking her head, she made her way around it and toward the back, where she found a back door and the light switches.

Flipping them into the 'on' position, she closed her eyes to lessen the shock of going from dark to bright. When she opened them, she saw she was facing the equivalent of a warehouse.

The room was massive. The first floor had been separated into two rooms of vastly different sizes, the front being the store, and the back was the stockroom. There were boxes on shelves and things hanging from the ceiling, as well as items in the aisles between the shelves stacked on top of each other.

Shaking her head, she made sure the back door was secure and turned to find the stairs.

I don't remember it being this cluttered when Tara showed me the place during the walk-through.

According to the listing, there was a fully furnished upstairs apartment, so Alice hoped that was correct because all she had were her keepsakes and clothes, and not even all of them. Alice had donated all her winter clothing in hopes of never having to wear her large parka again.

Opening the doors, she found the small office, complete with a desk, a filing cabinet overflowing with documents, and a safe.

Do I have the code for the safe?

Alice closed the door and found a broom closet filled with more odds and ends and cleaning supplies. There were only two doors left, and Alice really hoped one went to the stairs leading to the apartment.

The next door led to a small bathroom with a toilet and sink in desperate need of cleaning.

She opened the last door to find two sets of stairs, one going up and one going down.

Alice said aloud, "There was no mention of a basement. This is Florida. There shouldn't be a basement with the high-water table. I do *not* want to deal with flooding." The surprises kept on coming, so she took the stairs up to look at her new home.

At the top of the stairs, she gasped. Upstairs was nothing like downstairs, as it was light and airy versus dark and somewhat musty. There was minimal furniture, and everything was neatly arranged. She ran her fingertips over the marble countertop with and stainless-steel appliances in the kitchen as she ventured through the apartment. Large bay windows allowed the sun in to light the room.

The living room, dining room, and kitchen were in the center of the apartment, and the two bedrooms were on opposite sides. After inspecting both, she chose the one at the back of the building, even though both bedrooms were beautifully furnished with full bathrooms. The rear bedroom had a view of the alley behind the store. The back was noticeably quieter than the busy front because of a lack of foot traffic.

Through the rear bedroom window, she noticed a driveway at the back of her building.

Back on the first floor, she went to the rear of the building to see if she could find a door or access to the driveway she'd seen from upstairs. Shrugging at not seeing anything, it was time to check out the basement.

Alice didn't hate basements, but she wasn't a huge fan of them either. Nathan used to joke about buying a house with one just to give her a hard time, but thankfully, they never did.

Down in the basement, she turned on the light. She realized it was a walk-out basement, with two large doors at the back of the building. There was even already a car sitting in one of the two parking spaces.

Alice didn't know cars like she knew antiques, but she knew this one was old and in great shape. The rest of the space was filled to the ceiling with boxes neatly labeled with things like "Johnson estate" and "Christmas Antiques". Alice didn't know how much inventory to expect going into the purchase and almost felt bad for paying so little.

Scanning the room, she saw a pile of blinds she hoped were the right size to use upstairs on the front windows.

A scraping sound made Alice jump until she saw an old metal wind spinner in the corner, spinning slowly thanks to a previously unnoticed draft.

Stop being such a wuss. It's just a basement.

Turning off the lights, she went back upstairs and took an inventory of everything she needed to do. She had the hotel room for another four nights, but from the looks of the apartment upstairs, she could move in earlier than expected, allowing her to get more work done, faster.

The first thing she wanted to do was switch out the stained sheets covering the windows for something better. No one needed to see her sweating and singing along to 2000s metal music while cleaning the store.

The next morning, Alice started bright and early with buying everything she needed. Before going back to the store, she looked up the addresses of the electric and water companies. Thankfully, trash was paid for by the business district, so she didn't have to worry about it. First stop was the electric company.

***

"Hello, I need to switch service to my name on 10 Aviles Street, please."

The elderly lady glanced up at Alice from her computer screen. "Someone finally bought Old Man Morgan's place, huh? Have fun with that." She laughed as she brought up the information.

Alice was going to ask what she meant, but the lady looked back at her. "What's the name of the business?"

"Can it be in my personal name for the time being? I don't have a name finalized yet."

"No. Sorry, hun. It's in the commercial district and must have a business name. I can do a 'care of' with your name."

Without thinking, Alice spit out, "Forgotten Echoes Antiques store."

"Nice name. It looks like the power was already paid for this month, so you shouldn't be getting a bill until next month. I don't think the realtor expected it would sell so quickly – or at all." The lady laughed again, this time so hard she coughed.

"Thank you. Have a nice day," Alice said as she left the office.

What a strange lady.

The water company had a similar reaction when she said what property she'd bought.

Who is this Old Man Morgan?

She was so excited about the property and that everything had come back in such good condition, she didn't even think about looking at the history of the building. Then again, most of the buildings in Old Town St. Augustine were older than the 20th century and had stories to tell. Many of their histories weren't all rainbows and butterflies. In a town this old, there were bound to be some morbid endings.

Getting back to the store, she called the internet company. The realtor had said there hadn't been internet installed, but Alice wanted it. If nothing other than to make her life easier and the business more profitable by accepting credit cards. Few people carry cash or checks anymore.

"Hi, I need to start internet service at a property I recently bought," Alice stated as soon as someone answered the phone.

"What's the address?"

"10 Aviles Street." She waited for a snarky reply, or a laugh, but instead heard, "There is already internet service at that address. I can transfer it to your name. Would you like landline phone service as well?"

Alice was shocked. "Yes, I would.

"Perfect. Thank you." She wondered why the realtor hadn't known there was internet.

After handling the utilities, Alice decided her last goal for the day was to change out the sheets covering the windows, and she considered burning them.

Right before she flipped on the light switch in the basement, she thought she heard boxes being moved around, but when she turned on the light, everything looked the same.

Fantastic. I'm going crazy.

The blinds were behind both cars, so Alice maneuvered around both cars to measure the blinds.

Finding the blinds were a perfect fit, she loaded her arms with the panels and went back upstairs.

Once she finished installing the blinds, she moved all her personal items upstairs from her car. Gazing out the window at the streetlights, she decided it was a good time to have a tea and read a book before going to bed.

Reaching a good stopping point, Alice put her empty teacup into the sink and went back to her room to sleep. Right as she dozed off, she heard someone say, *Don't let him have it.* It was muffled, so she assumed it was coming from outside and rolled over before going to sleep.

Chapter Four

"Damn it. The minute I have the money, I'm putting in a dumbwaiter." Alice kicked a box of books. She'd spent the last three days cleaning and organizing.

Unfortunately, she'd gone downstairs to the basement and found several books she thought would be perfect, only for them to weigh the same as a baby elephant.

Giving up on organizing the items, she went into the office and tried to see what was going on there. The internet company had dropped a single line near the cash register so she could take cards. Occasionally, she heard whispering voices, but this area of St. Augustine was pretty loud most of the time as far as she'd noticed, so she brushed it off.

The code to the safe had been found inside a drawer, so she opened it to find it full of random items. She shook her head and closed it again.

That's for another day, or week.

She heard the jingle of the bell over the front door, letting her know someone had come into the store.

Weird. I thought I'd locked it.

She left the office using a bandana to wipe her face.

A short, pudgy man was making his way toward her.

She couldn't see his entire face because he wore a fedora and was looking at the floor.

"I'm sorry. We aren't open yet. That door was locked."

"That doesn't matter. I'm here for a specific item, and I'd like to purchase it before anyone else can."

Don't let him have it. It sounded like someone was whispering in her ear.

"Who's there?" Alice tried to find the voice, but no one else was there.

"Who said what?" The man glared at her.

"Nothing. I thought I heard something. You're saying you broke into my store to buy something?" Alice couldn't believe what she was hearing. Tara must have put someone up to this.

"Clearly. Now, I must have it."

"Why don't you take a look around? Perhaps you can find it and if you do, I can sell it to you. As you can see, this place isn't in the greatest shape. I'm still —"

"I don't want your excuses. I need it right now." The man slammed both hands on the countertop. One finger had a ring with a triangle pressed into the top of it.

"Sir, I don't mean to sound grumpy, but I've been working all day. I have no earthly idea what you're looking for."

Don't let him have it. Tell him to leave.

This time, when Alice heard the voice, she didn't flinch.

"Sir, I think it's time for you to leave."

"I'm not leaving without it. Now find it!" the man yelled at her.

She reached for the phone hanging on the wall.

"One last chance before I call the cops. Or if you tell me what you're looking for, I can help you look for it. I may not even have it. Or you can leave now."

"Fine, I'm leaving, but I'll be back, and you will give it to me when I return."

"Sure thing. Considering I don't know what you're looking for, I'm sure that's exactly what'll happen." Alice rolled her eyes as the man left.

Thank you.

"Who is speaking to me? You come out and answer me right now."

It is I, Kyle Morgan, the owner of this store.

"You need to stop. Kyle Morgan has been dead for who knows how long. I bought the store free and clear. I want to know where the speaker is, and who set you up to do this. It was Tara, wasn't it?"

Ugh Women.

A faint outline of a man materialized in front of Alice, two feet from where the pudgy man had been standing.

She dropped her phone and stepped back. "Who the —? what the —?"

"Calm down before you give yourself a heart attack."

"Who are you?"

As the figure materialized a bit more, she could see him roll his eyes.

"Um, I can see through you. Who are you?"

Stretching, the figure observed her. "I'm Kyle Morgan, like I said. I'm the previous owner of this business."

"And why are you still here?"

"I don't rightly know, but I can guess."

"Then can you guess?"

"Death entrusted me with some items before I died."

"Death, as in the Grim Reaper?" Alice could not believe she was talking to what appeared to be a ghost.

"You know someone else who goes by Death? But he doesn't like being called Death. He prefers to go by another name. Nice guy, likes blue."

"This 'Death' gave you things? Why? That make no sense."

"It doesn't matter right now. I'm sure Death will introduce himself to you soon enough. So how much did you pay for my store?" the ghost of Kyle Morgan questioned her.

"Three hundred thousand because I bought it quickly."

"Isn't that a hoot? You bought it from my good-for-nothing family for less than I have in inventory. How did you pull the money together so quickly? I know the sale was likely cash, right?" He wandered around the store.

"My husband died a year ago, and his life insurance policy was more than enough. Yes, the sale was all cash. They said they wanted to sell it as quickly as possible."

"I'm sorry to hear of your loss."

"Um, Mr. Morgan, is there something I can do for you?" All the hard work she'd been doing must have finally made her hallucinate. With a building this old, Alice wondered if it was arsenic or lead.

"The guy who just left? His name is Trent Benson, high lord of something. You *cannot* let him take anything from this store."

"Why? I mean, if he has the money —."

"NO."

Alice felt the vibration as he yelled.

"What we are *not* going to do, is yell. Excuse me while I go upstairs and eat dinner." She turned her back on the ghost faced toward the stairs. She didn't know if it would work, but it had always worked on her husband and daughter, so why not try it on Kyle?

"I'm sorry. He's just a terrible person, and I don't want him to have whatever he's demanding. Death told me he would come asking for it."

"Where is this 'thing' he's looking for?" Alice stood, tapping her toe.

"See, one minor issue; I don't remember."

"You know what? Let's pick this up tomorrow." Alice figured it was all in her head, and he wouldn't be there in the morning.

"Fine, but please help me."

"Yes, tomorrow." Alice made sure the front door was locked and turned off the lights.

I should probably get those locks changed. Who knows who has a key?

She closed the door on the first floor and the one upstairs. Alice knew little about ghosts. Who was she kidding? She knew nothing about ghosts, but hopefully closing the doors would stop any ghosts or whatever was downstairs from coming up.

***

The next morning, Alice remembered the company she hired to make the new sign would be there at ten. Since her alarm had just dinged, she knew it was 8:30, giving her enough time to eat and look over the awakening town from the front bedroom window. She had decided the front bedroom would be her office, while she would use the office downstairs to store valuables since the safe was in there.

Downstairs, she didn't see anything, but as she turned away from the front door.

I'm still here, and you said you would help. Kyle Morgan's voice carried through the room.

"Stop doing whatever you're doing. What do you need help with?" Alice shouted at the empty room. As she passed the counter with the register, she saw the image materializing by the stairs.

"I need to keep certain objects out of certain people's hands. You were chosen to buy this place."

"What? No, I wasn't. My daughter saw it online."

"You can see ghosts. You were destined to own it."

"Listen, I don't know what kind of game this is, but if I can see ghosts, why can't I see my Nathan?" Alice almost broke down in tears.

The image shrugged. "Could be he moved on, or you aren't ready? I don't know how this whole ghost thing works; I'm new to it too."

"New to talking to one or new to being one?"

"Ouch, that stung. Being one. I could talk to ghosts before I became one."

"I guess I'm not the only crazy person … ghost … entity standing in the room."

"Just calm down."

"You know, telling someone to calm down rarely works." Alice paced the room. "Great, I'm expected to protect these 'items' for Death. Who goes by another name?"

"Yes."

"Do you know what this other name is?"

"No idea. I only saw him a couple times."

"Fantastic. You're just a fountain of information, aren't you? What am I supposed to do? Sit here and wait around for this 'Death' to arrive?"

He looked like he was contemplating the question. "No, I think there's a list of stuff Death has given me to protect for the right person somewhere in my office."

"You couldn't have … I don't know … left a note?" Alice felt like she was losing her mind, arguing with a ghost — or someone who called himself a ghost.

"I didn't know I was going to die."

"But you have a list of everything Death told you to keep safe?"

"Exactly."

Alice shook her head. "Welp, let's find this list."

For the next hour, she dug through paperwork on the desk while Kyle stood next to her, being unhelpful, telling her when something wasn't what she was looking for.

"You know what, Kyle? Why don't I open the safe and see if the list or the item is in there?"

"It won't be."

Alice wanted to strangle him. Her cell phone rang as she opened her mouth to yell at him.

"Hello?" she greeted as it connected.

"Hi, I have your sign ready for you."

"Great, I'll open the front door." Alice clicked off and looked at Kyle. "You stay here." She didn't wait for him to respond as she went to the front door and unlocked it. Stepping through, she saw the large sign and two men holding it.

"Where do you want it?"

"Right here." Alice pointed to the space above the door and below the upstairs windows. There were already hooks for a sign.

"Awesome. We'll get this up right now." The two men got to work as Alice turned and saw Kyle standing behind them.

"Can you see someone standing behind you?" Alice asked them.

The men looked behind them. "No, there's no one there. You okay?" The one in the blue hat gave her a side-eye.

"Yeah, I thought I saw something. It's been a morning. I'll leave you to it."

Back inside the store, Alice closed the door, leaning against it.

"You don't have a brain tumor, I told you. You're destined for this."

"How about we don't read my mind, mmkay? I'm a widow from Oregon. How can I possibly be destined for this?"

Kyle shrugged as he moved around the store.

"Thanks. That's helpful. I guess I should get back to hauling inventory up to the store from the basement."

"Why are you bringing things up?"

"Because it will sell?"

"Be careful."

"What? With carrying objects?" Alice watched Kyle, who was trying to touch a plate, but his hand kept going through it.

"Yes, and there are things down there which should stay down there." Kyle gave up on the plate and went over to a picture of the main gates of St. Augustine.

"Like what? Because all I've seen so far is random crap and books too heavy to carry up here. How did you carry stuff up here at your age?" Alice regarded him. She didn't know how old Kyle was when he died, but he seemed to be around 80 years old.

"The dumbwaiter I had installed when I turned 55."

"You have a damn dumbwaiter, and here I was carrying crap upstairs. Where is it?" Alice went toward the stairs.

She didn't get a response. At the bottom of the stairs to the basement, she searched for where it could possibly be. Deeper into the room, she saw Kyle's figure attempting to lean against a wall, just past the car.

"Kyle, you're dead. You can't touch or lean on things anymore."

"Dead is a state of mind. If I work at it hard enough, eventually I'll be able to."

Right, and I'll lose 50 pounds and start running every day. Alice laughed to herself.

"So where is this magical dumbwaiter?"

"Right here." He motioned to what she'd thought was an electrical box.

Opening the door, she saw it was, in fact, a shaft with controls right inside the door. She peeked inside.

"You can put your head in there. It isn't moving, so it won't cut your head off." Kyle stood right next to her.

Alice yipped as she glared at him but stuck her head inside. Looking up to see it went quite a ways before she saw the bottom of the dumbwaiter car.

Pulling her head out, she looked at Kyle. "You know, there's a lot of stuff your realtor didn't know about this property."

"Obviously, since they only sold it for 300,000." Kyle tried to kick a box full of light sconces, but his foot went through.

Before she could respond, she heard her phone ringing and realized she had left it on the counter upstairs, so she went up and grabbed it.

"Hello?"

"Hi, Ms. Tidway. This is Tony from outside. We're finished if you want to come check it out."

"Great. I'll be out in a minute."

Not bothering to ask Kyle to stay, Alice went outside to see her new sign.

"Forgotten Echoes. It's got a nice ring to it. Much better than 'Morgan's Antiques'," Kyle commented next to her.

Alice almost responded before she remembered no one else could see Kyle.

"It looks great, guys. Thank you."

"Thank you, Ms. Tidway. If you have any issues with it, let me know, and I'll come see what I can do." Tony shook Alice's hand before motioning to the other man to gather up their tools, and they left.

As she closed the door, she looked around for anything obviously needing to be done.

"We need to find your list," Kyle said.

Alice jumped, still not used to the fact she could see and hear a ghost.

"We will, but first, why was your family so eager to get rid of this place??"

"Probably because they didn't want to deal with the property since none of those worthless good-for-nothings can see ghosts." Kyle was nonchalant about his insults.

Alice stopped and stared at him. "What do you mean, ghost-S?"

"You thought I was the only ghost here? Nah, there are a bunch."

"I didn't sign up for ghosts. I didn't sign up for even one ghost."

"Now that you can see me, you can't really unopen the bottle."

"What do you mean? I could go back to Oregon and put the store back on the market. Or I could rent out the apartment until it sells."

"It'll never sell, and you could, but you'd still see ghosts."

"How are you so sure? I thought you didn't know how it worked?" Alice put her hands on her hips.

"I tried the same thing when I first bought this place."

Alice mulled over what she had learned. "You know what? I'm done for the day." She locked the front door and before she took a step up the stairs, she eyed Kyle. "You stay here."

Upstairs in her apartment, she traced her steps to the area where she thought the dumbwaiter shaft should be. It took her running into walls between the living room and the bedroom, but she thought she found it.

Opening the door, it wasn't the dumbwaiter, but a simple closet. Toward the back of the closet, she saw a seam with a small handle showing there was a door, hopefully to the dumbwaiter shaft.

I need to do more research on dumbwaiters. Why did I think an entire door would exist for a small dumbwaiter? I must be the dumb one.

Grabbing the small handle, she twisted it open.

Well, Well, Well. A dumbwaiter will make life so much easier.

Inside the door were two small buttons, one with an arrow pointing up and one with an arrow pointing down. The dumbwaiter car was already on her floor, and her bedroom lighting made it much easier to see inside, so she could see the light glimmering off something.

When she touched the glimmering object, a jolt of electricity ran up her arm. Dropping it, she shook out her hand and tentatively touched it again. She felt as if she was drawn to it. This time, she felt nothing, so she picked up the pocket watch. Pulling it out, she looked at both sides. One side was plain, while the other had a symbol resembling two misshapen triangles facing away from each other.

"What's that?" Kyle asked.

Alice jumped and dropped the watch on the floor.

"I thought I told you to stay on the first floor or in the basement. Really, anywhere but here."

"You did, but it got lonely. I wanted to see what they did with the place." Kyle meandered around the apartment.

"You've been dead, what? Three months? And now, suddenly, you're lonely?"

"It's not like I was popular before I died. So, yeah. I was lonely."

"You might think it's all well and good, but this is my house now, and I would appreciate if you didn't pop in and out whenever you please."

"Sorry. I won't do it again. Unless it's important."

"What could possibly be important to you?" Alice reached for the pocket watch she had dropped.

"You never know. Like you finding an old pocket watch. That's something that could be important to me."

"Kyle, spit it out. I don't like games."

"You own an antiques store; you must like *some* games."

"Puzzles but stop. I'm hungry. I had a long day, and I don't need more from you."

"How about you set the pocket watch on the table, and I'll check it out while you make yourself something to eat?" Kyle shrugged.

She opened the watch to find two black and white photos, one of a woman, and the other a man. They looked to be in their forties. Placing the open watch on the table, she went back to close the doors. Closing the door, she returned and saw Kyle staring at the images.

"Can you turn it over?" Kyle asked as she was finishing putting her soup on the stove.

"Sure, here." Flipping it over, she returned to the stove to stir the chicken noodle soup.

"Interesting."

"What's interesting?"

"I've seen this marking before, but I don't remember where. You eat; I'll try to remember where I've seen it."

Before Alice could say anything, he was gone.

Taking her bowl to the table, she felt tired as she looked at the pocket watch. She closed her eyes just for a second.

"Alice, wake up!" Alice was jolted awake by Kyle's yelling.

"What? I didn't fall asleep."

"You did."

Alice looked down at her soup and took a bite, only to find it ice cold.

"How did that happen?"

"Stress, all the work you've done around here, this watch, staring at my beautiful face. All those things combined could make someone tired."

"Dealing with you could definitely make me tired."

"Why, you wound me, Alice."

Rolling her eyes, Alice put her soup back in the microwave and turned to Kyle.

"Did you find anything while I was napping?"

"I did. Do you want to know about it now?"

"Let's do it tomorrow." Alice yawned as she heard the store phone ring.

Kyle shrugged.

Jogging downstairs, she got to the phone on the fifth ring. She should probably get a voicemail set up.

Wait, how did anyone get this number?

Expecting it to be telemarketers, she answered, "Forgotten Echoes."

"Did you find it yet?" a gravelly male voice asked.

"Did I find what yet? Who is this?"

The man didn't answer her questions. He commanded, "You'd better find it," and hung up. Alice held the phone for a minute, staring at it in disbelief before setting it back onto the cradle.

"Who was on the phone?"

"Some man asking if I'd 'found it'."

"Wonder if it was Trent. I bet he'll show up tomorrow. Speaking of tomorrow, when do you want to reopen the store?" Kyle asked next to her.

"Why? You going to help?" Alice was too tired and creeped out by the phone call to care anymore.

"I totally will. I can let you know where things are if someone comes looking for something not up front."

"How about you find the so-called list you had, and I'll handle the customers?"

"Fine, fine. I'll see you tomorrow."

"Don't come creeping in at night while I'm asleep. Is there, like, ghost repellent?"

"I promise I won't." Kyle was gone and Alice missed his presence. It was nice having someone to talk to. Not that she would admit it.

Up in her kitchen, she looked sadly at her cold soup and shook her head. Deciding to forego dinner, she took her phone, hoping tomorrow would be better because today had been a mess.

While she still thought she was probably hallucinating Kyle, and it was from the stress of moving, she was coming around to having a ghost, maybe.

I am absolutely going to get checked to see if I have a brain tumor

She considered going back into the kitchen for tea but was so exhausted she decided it wasn't worth it.

Chapter Five

Alice started the next day thinking about what she wanted to accomplish. The store was improving, but there was a long way to go before she felt it was ready for customers.

As much as she didn't believe in Death or ghosts, Kyle was making her believe a little. But not enough to tell Tara about it.

While her tea brewed, she made a list of how to get the store ready. The grand opening was this weekend, just three days away, and it wasn't ready. She knew she could do it. Assuming random strangers didn't keep barging in to the shop, uninvited.

She added, 'find the list supposedly Death gave to Kyle' to the list to humor him. She also wanted to organize all the random stuff in the basement and stockroom so she could find it more easily.

Thinking about how she would go about gathering more items once she sold her current stock, her kettle whistled. Pouring it into a large travel cup, she ate her yogurt and went downstairs.

On the first floor, all she could hear was yelling. It sounded like it was coming from the front of the store, but she knew she had locked the front door. Approaching the door, she moved the shade back to see Kyle arguing with a man outside the door as tourists walked through them, unaware.

Opening the door and waiting for a break in tourists, she whisper-yelled at Kyle, "Get in here!"

Kyle noticed her and sheepishly came inside, with the man following. After making sure the door was locked and the shade back in place, she turned to the men, who glared at each other.

"It's too early in the morning for me to have to deal with this." She motioned between them.

"It wasn't my fault. I was looking for the thing you asked me to look for, and this man showed up."

"I didn't just show up, you twit."

"Well, you weren't here, and then you were, so obviously you showed up." Kyle and the man argued again.

"Stop." Alice sat in the chair she had moved from the basement to the store just yesterday. She stared at them as she drank her tea.

"What's going on?"

When Kyle opened his mouth to speak, she raised her finger, telling Kyle to stop so Alistair could speak. It worked to stop Nathan and Tara from fighting, so she figured it couldn't hurt to try it on them.

"I'm sorry for bothering you, ma'am. But I was in limbo, and then suddenly I was here." The man sheepishly removed his hat.

"What do you mean? You know what? Never mind. Kyle, why are you so upset about this?"

"Not all ghosts are good, and he looks shady to me." Kyle folded his arms over his chest.

Alice stifled the laugh.

Kyle, a ghost, calling another ghost shady? You can't get better comedy.

"And you are?"

"I'm Alistair."

"Are you from around here? Why would you have come here?" Alice asked him.

"No, I'm from Ohio, and I've never been here before," Alistair offered as Kyle glared at him.

Alice couldn't believe she was talking to not one, but two ghosts.

"Why were you fighting?"

"Because I don't believe him," Kyle stomped by.

"Look, Alistair, I don't know why you're here. But unless you figure it out, I don't know if I can help you." Alice stood and moved to the counter.

Alistair looked down in sadness, but suddenly, his head shot up in excitement. "I think I remember something."

Alice and Kyle narrowed their eyes at the same time.

"Oh? Why are you here?"

"A pocket watch. My daughter moved to Florida, and I think she had it when she died. It might have ended up here."

"Florida is a big state. Why would you think it was here?"

"I'm here, right? It must be in your shop."

"You're more than welcome to look at the jewelry we have. We don't have much right now, though."

"Thank you. I'm sure you have it." Alistair moved toward the glass cabinet where the jewelry was kept.

Alice caught Kyle's eye and motioned upstairs before he disappeared.

In seconds, he was back and nodding, which to Alice meant the pocket watch they'd found in the dumbwaiter was still there.

She joined the man at the cabinet. "Is it here?"

"No, I don't see it." The man looked sad but also slightly angry.

"I have an entire stockroom full of stuff I haven't had a chance to go through yet. Can you tell me what the watch looked like? This way, if I find it, I can save it for you?"

"It was gold, oval, and I think it had symbols on the front."

That really narrows it down.

"Do you know what kind of symbols?" Alice already knew what the man was going to say.

"It was, like, two triangles interlocking. Sorry, I haven't seen it in so long."

Yeah, I bet you haven't.

"I think I understand. What was your daughter's name? I'm getting into the files the previous owner left behind. I can keep a watch out for her name."

"Um. I don't know what her married name was, but I know she was married." The man's eyes darted back and forth like he wanted to run away.

"Fine. What was her first name?" Alice didn't feel bad for this ghost at all. She had a feeling he was involved with the man who had come in previously, and she wanted as much information as she could get. Even if the information was fake.

"Meredith," the man finally said.

"I'll keep an eye out for the name and for an estate which had a pocket watch. In the meantime, I apologize, but I need you to leave the store. I have a list of things I need to accomplish."

"I understand. When should I check back again?"

"How about next week after the grand opening? If I find it, I'll make sure it doesn't get put out with everything else."

"Alright. I guess I'll be going." The man vanished before her eyes.

"Kyle?" Alice called out.

"Yes?" His voice came from right behind her, and she jumped.

"Don't do that again."

"Don't do what?" Kyle grinned.

"Is he gone?" Alice studied the surrounding area.

"He is."

"You think he was looking for the same thing we just found?" Alice was suspicious.

"It's strange because when he first appeared here, he had a completely different story."

"Did you find the list while I was talking to Alistair?"

"No, I was checking the dumbwaiter. I found something else which may interest you." Kyle tapped his foot, waiting for her.

Finishing her tea, she left the mug on the counter as she followed him back.

"Remember how it had a weird symbol on it? I found a puzzle box with the same symbols."

It was as if neither of them wanted to mention the words 'pocket watch,' in case Alistair was still roaming about.

He stopped near a shelf and pointed at a cardboard box pushed all the way to the back.

Alice pulled it out and looked inside. It was full of knick-knacks, and at the very bottom was a wooden box with the same two triangles on the top.

"Isn't this interesting …" Alice looked at the box. It was solid, or at least appeared solid.

"I think it's a puzzle box." Kyle watched her look over it.

"I think you're right. Do you remember anything about this box?"

"Here's the thing…" Kyle wouldn't look Alice in the eye.

"What?"

"Items just kinda show up here sometimes … by themselves."

"Yeah, you buy things, they arrive. Do you mean something different?"

"When I was alive, I would have this place completely cleared out, and the next morning it would be full of merchandise again. I don't know where it all came from."

"So, I'm talking to a ghost … inside a shop … which finds stuff to sell all by itself?"

"Exactly." Kyle grinned.

Alice groaned. This was not what she had planned for her move to Florida.

"You'll make good money."

"Oh, I will?"

"Yep, items people want to buy appear, but then other times there are things sitting here for a while as it collects dust."

"Not helpful, Kyle. Not helpful at all. You know what? I'm going to pretend there aren't a bunch of living and dead people who probably want the same thing, and act like this is an ordinary business."

"Good luck," Kyle called out before he disappeared.

Alice took the puzzle box upstairs and put it next to the pocket watch in the dumbwaiter. She didn't know why two seemingly different men wanted it, but it was best to have them away from prying eyes. A nagging feeling in Alice's stomach told her Trent and Alistair were somehow connected.

Alice thought of something on her way downstairs.

"Kyle?"

"Yes?" This time, Kyle was across the room.

"Did Death mention if there were any safe and secure places in this building where it would be good to keep his items?"

"You mean somewhere where a ghost couldn't see?"

"Exactly."

Kyle cocked his head as if he was trying to remember. "You know, I think he put something about it on the list he gave me."

"Kyle, I'm going to strangle you. Are you sure this magical list is somewhere?"

"It's in the office. I'm sure of it."

"Whatever." Even though cleaning the office wasn't high on her list for today, Alice went into the small room and worked on organizing.

As the day progressed, she was getting frustrated because she found a lot of receipts and inventory lists, but nothing resembling a random list written by Death. How did Death write, anyway? Was it gothic print?

"Here it is." Kyle pointed at a piece of paper sitting in a drawer Alice had just opened.

"Finally." Alice picked it up and read over it. It was regular print handwriting, and part of her was disappointed it wasn't fancier. If she was going to believe in ghosts and Death himself, then she hoped he'd be fancy.

The list wasn't long; it only had two items on it. Slapping it onto the desk, she turned to Kyle, unimpressed. "This list has two things on it."

"No, it doesn't. It has" — Kyle counted the lines on the page — "twenty things."

"Well, genius, apparently I can only see two of them."

"Which two?"

"A pocket watch and a puzzle box." Alice thought about what she'd said and looked harder at the list. Nothing else appeared. "Maybe it is only the things I have seen so far?"

"Just so you know, I can see there's a bunch of stuff listed on it. Why don't you try asking it?" Kyle grinned like a kid in a candy store.

"What? You want me to talk to a piece of paper?"

"The paper probably doesn't trust you."

"Kyle, I'm about to toss this piece of paper out the window and find someone who can get rid of you." Alice was frustrated by the whole situation and wanted to be done with it.

"Just ask it."

"Fine, but when nothing else comes up, I'm done with this whole secret item crap. The ghost and the short guy can have whatever it is they want." Alice rolled her eyes at what she was about to do, but she still focused on the paper. "Show me the full list." Expecting nothing to happen, she was about to tell Kyle that it was a failure, until he pointed at the paper.

"Where is a safe place to hide secrets?" Alice figured it if worked the first time, it should work the second.

The dumbwaiter holds secrets safe.

"Looks like I was right."

"I. Will. Stab. You." Alice read the list on the paper she held. Shaking her head, she dropped the note and went upstairs.

Out of curiosity, she opened the dumbwaiter to make sure there wasn't anything else inside. Sitting right where she left them were the watch and the box. Closing the door, she leaned against the closet door.

She went downstairs and inspected the list again. Feeling stupid, she asked it, "Show me the rest of the list of items I need to keep safe."

Immediately, a handwritten list of items appeared on the paper.

"A tackle box?" Alice questioned the list.

"I remember when it came in. It's supposed to go somewhere near the Pacific Coast. Death told me under no circumstances should I sell it as individual pieces. It must be sold together."

"What? Was it owned by some great fisherman?" Alice laughed at Kyle's expression.

"I don't know. Death didn't tell me, but I figured it must be important."

Just then, Alice felt a hot flash coming on. They weren't common yet, but she had them occasionally. Sitting, she fanned herself.

"Are you okay?" Kyle stood near the door. "You aren't sick, are you?"

"It isn't like you could catch it if I was? But no, I'm not sick. I'm a 45-year-old woman," Alice quipped back.

"What does that — ohh, my wife experienced those."

"You were married?"

"I was. It was my damn grandkids who sold you this property, or possibly my son. He was always my least favorite."

Alice wanted to laugh but could see Kyle wasn't happy about the store being sold.

"Why do you think they sold it?"

"Probably because they all thought I was crazy when I told them I could see and talk to ghosts, but none of them could. I assumed it was something genetic to be passed down through the generations, but I guess not."

He gestured to Alice.

"How much do you know about our special gift?" Alice's hot flash had passed, so she was going through paperwork, careful to place the list of things to be saved on top of the safe before moving stuff.

"From what Death has said, a child is born every 30 years with the gift, give or take. Sometimes they open stores like this or take over an existing one. Other times, they become psychics. My great-grandmother, Edna, worked as a tarot card reader for the circus before they moved to Florida."

"Interesting. Is it safe to assume it isn't only one family?"

"Not really sure. I've never met anyone else outside of my great grandmother, but if you're 45, then you can't be from my line. My kids are in their late 70s, and I know all their kids."

"Let's put a pin in where I got my ghost talking. Why didn't it start until now?"

Kyle shrugged. "Don't know. I've had it my whole life. Imagine being a 10-year-old talking to your friendly neighbor, only to find out later they'd died before you were born. Let's just say I didn't have many friends. I learned to not mention around anyone and tried to ignore it until I opened this store. Could it be it started when you moved down?"

"Not really helpful, but I guess there isn't a newsletter I can join that shares that kind of information."

"There is, actually. Death told me about it. I don't remember the name now, but I bet it's online versus the old paper copies I used to get."

I cannot believe there's a ghost communication newsletter.

"The office is looking somewhat better now. Seriously, if stock just shows up on its own, why do you have so much paperwork?"

"You'd be surprised. I kept everything because sometimes things had a way of returning themselves."

"Great. Did the customer get an automatic refund too?" Alice laughed as Kyle considered it.

"I don't think so, but I don't rightly know, now that you mention it." Kyle's answer was serious, which made Alice laugh even more.

"I'm going crazy. It's the only logical explanation for any of this." Alice spoke more to herself than to Kyle.

"No, you aren't, but with less than three whole days until you open, we should get going with the store."

"You're right. Let me put this note in the safe and lock it up." Alice closed the safe and turned off the light before going back to the front.

"It looks good so far."

"I agree, but you're going to need to clean up the stockroom. When I ran the store, I was constantly running from the front to the back. It was exhausting," Kyle suggested.

"I should probably get started."

For the rest of the day, Alice worked on organizing the back. However, every time she finished clearing or organizing a shelf, more items needing to be sorted appeared.

"Does it ever stop?"

"No, but you get used to it." Kyle smiled as he looked in the newest box. "You should see what's in this one."

Among the candle holders and paper weights, inside the box was a jewelry box. It had the same symbols as the pocket watch and the puzzle box, but this one opened easily.

Inside, she found a ring and a necklace. Pulling out the ring, it was similar to the one Trent, the first man, had worn. The small flower pendant on the necklace had a clear gem in the center. She wasn't sure if it was a diamond or something else.

Alice consulted Kyle. "I think these should probably go into the dumbwaiter as well."

"I agree." Kyle went over to the dumbwaiter and tried to open it.

"Why did you try to open it? You can't actually touch anything."

"Not yet, but I have a feeling the closer we get to the grand opening, the more I'll be able to do. I figured I might as well keep trying until it happens."

"You do, do you?"

"What have I got to lose?"

Opening the door, Alice placed the items next to the puzzle box before pushing them all the way to the back.

"Hey, the car in the basement? Was it yours?"

"I wish. It showed up full of stuff. There's a key around here somewhere."

"Fantastic. Another surprise." Alice was fascinated by what was happening, while also growing tired of always having something new occur or show up to be dealt with. She thought buying the antiques store might help her get over Nathan's death, as well as occupy her time. Now, it was shaping up to be a full-time job on top of talking to ghosts and keeping things secret.

Not the experience I was looking for, but apparently the one I got. I hope you're laughing, Nathan.

Alice was saddened by the fact she could talk to ghosts, but not to the one ghost she truly wanted to. Shrugging, she brushed her hands off and got back to work cleaning up the shelves.

Later that evening as she prepared dinner, she pulled out her laptop and searched for the symbol on the jewelry and boxes.

She thought she'd found what she was searching for right as the oven dinged. As she stood, the store phone rang downstairs. Quickly pulling her food out of the oven, she rushed downstairs.

"Forgotten Echoes, Alice speaking." Alice was met with silence. "Hello?"

Just as she was about to hang up, dismissing the call as a wrong number, a quiet voice said, "He will get it, and there's nothing you can do about it." The phone clicked when they hung up.

On her way upstairs, she wondered what the caller could have meant. Shaking her head, she plated her food and moved over to the table to continue her search.

"Who was on the phone?"

"No one at first, but then someone said, 'he will get it, and there's nothing you can do about it.' I have no idea what they're talking about."

"Think it has to do with the items in the dumbwaiter?" Kyle asked, floating around in Alice's head.

"Possibly, but it could've also been someone pranking the store. Or worse, someone trying to scare me."

"Perhaps. You never know, though." Kyle moved to see what was on Alice's computer screen.

"An unicursal hexagram, huh." Alice pointed to the symbol.

"A what?" Kyle's voice floated in from the living room.

"Weren't you just standing next to me?"

"I heard something and wanted to check it out."

"The call has you spooked, doesn't it?"

"No, but it isn't like I have much else to do. I can only go about ten feet from the building in any direction. There isn't any live music nearby tonight, either."

"Since you're here, do you want to read this with me while I eat?" Alice turned her laptop to the side so he could also see it.

"Looks a lot like the symbols we've seen, but what does it mean?"

"It looks like it's part of the Thelema religious movement. I've never heard of it before, have you?"

Kyle shook his head.

Alice pulled up the Wikipedia page for the Thelema spiritual philosophy and skimmed it.

"It looks like a pretty low-key religion. They're all about self-awareness, learning about your own true will, and being good to people."

"Definitely the same symbol, and the center looks like the flower and gem on the necklace. If this is what they're looking for, why?" Kyle commented as Alice moved the laptop back once she was done with dinner.

"And why was Death so adamant you keep it safe until the 'right person' comes along? I assume neither the ghost nor the man are the 'right people'?"

"I don't think so. Especially not the ghost; he gives me the creeps."

"Kyle, how does a ghost give another ghost the creeps?" Alice pursed her lips to keep from laughing.

"Look, I don't know everything, but I know he's no good."

"I don't disagree with you. I just think it's funny." Alice raised her hands.

"Maybe it is a *little* funny. Now that we've figured it out, I should get back downstairs so you can do whatever it is you do at night." Kyle waved as he disappeared.

Alice spent the next two hours sifting through the history and practices of Thelemism. Nothing stood out as odd or dangerous, but she had a feeling in her gut something wasn't quite right about the two men. Technically, it was a living man and a ghost.

Her eyes tired from staring at the computer screen, she made herself a cup of tea and settled in to read a book. Drifting off to sleep, she thought about Nathan and hoped he would come to her in her dreams. She had so much to tell him.

***

Unfortunately, when she woke, she realized she hadn't dreamed at all, or if she had, she didn't remember it. She always remembered her dreams with Nathan, so she knew he hadn't come. Her brain must be so tired with everything going on, it didn't need to conjure him up, or maybe it was because she wasn't in Oregon. She felt sad about the idea, especially if it meant she would never see him in her dreams again.

She couldn't worry about it now. All morning, she'd felt something was going to happen. Nothing seemed any different from usual when she got to the first floor. Setting up what she'd planned to doing today, her feelings came true.

This time, instead of ghosts fighting or a random person breaking in, it was half the lights burning out.

"Kyle, do you have anything to do with this?" Alice used the flashlight on her cellphone to navigate.

"Nope. Happened about an hour ago. You might want to call an electrician," Kyle offered.

"Thanks, I will. After I check the breaker box. Speaking of which, where's the breaker box?"

"In the basement."

"Of course it is. Thanks."

Alice worked her way down to the basement, mentally reminding herself she needed to buy a better flashlight. Tripping on multiple things as she followed Kyle's horrible directions, she found the metal breaker box. As she flipped the breakers off and then on, light flooded the room. Closing the cover, a newspaper on top of the box caught her eye. The picture on the front looked familiar, so she grabbed it and took it upstairs.

"No electrician needed." Kyle smiled at her as she passed by on her way to the counter.

"I'm handy. Anyway, look what I found downstairs. Does this look familiar?" Alice held up the paper.

"Isn't he the ghost who was here yesterday? Alistair?"

"Exactly what I was thinking. He's younger in this photo but definitely looks like the same guy." Alice opened the newspaper on the counter.

"What's he doing?" Kyle pointed at the picture.

"Grand Marshal of the Parade, it looks like." Alice shrugged.

"Where?"

"You can read as well as I can, Kyle." Alice side-eyed him.

"Sometimes I forget. Let me see it." Kyle stepped closer while Alice turned the paper around, so it was facing him.

"Palm Coast Florida's starlight parade with your Grand Marshal Alistair Sinclair." Kyle read the caption under the photo. "I thought Alistair said he was from Ohio."

"He did, and the newspaper is fairly recent, but I don't remember seeing it down there when I was moving things around."

"What a rat. I knew he was lying." Kyle went to slam the newspaper with his palm, but his hand went through the counter. "I told you, stuff shows up here all the time. You think I liked the shop always looking like a flea market stand? It was nice and organized, and then I met Death, and it went downhill from there."

"Death did all this?" Alice motioned to everything.

"I don't know if he did it or what, but yeah. I met Death, and then my shop started collecting stuff."

"Strange. Well, it is what it is, right? Let's make the best of it."

"I still don't trust Alistair." Kyle went back to looking around the front of the store.

"I don't trust either of them. Let's get this all straightened out for the grand opening." Alice folded the newspaper and placed it on a small shelf by the cash register.

***

For the rest of the day, Alice organized and made sure everything was ready for the open house scheduled in two days. Her goal was to get everything set up so she could take a day off before the grand opening.

While making dinner, her phone rang.

"Hey, Tara. How are you?"

"I'm good. How's the cleaning and organizing going?"

"It's going. There's a lot of stuff to get through, and with the grand opening coming up, I think I'm at a place where I can take the day off."

"Do you have anyone to help you?"

Alice couldn't tell Tara she could talk to ghosts, and it wasn't like Kyle would be much help. "No, not really, but I don't think it'll be too busy, you know?"

"I hope it's *really* busy. I think it'll help you. What are you doing tomorrow?"

"I'm going to get my hair done, or at least find somewhere to get my hair done. Alice sighed.

"Is everything alright" Tara heard her mom sigh.

"It's just been really busy and with everything going on, I miss your dad."

"I miss him too. Sorry if I pushed you too hard to do this. I thought it would be good for you."

"It *is* good for me, Tara. I needed to get out of Oregon, and this is a good thing. I promise you."

"Okay, I need to get to the gate for security. If you need anything, let me know."

"I will. Love you." Alice told her daughter.

"Love you too, Mom," Tara replied as she hung up.

It was one of their shorter conversations, but Alice enjoyed talking to her daughter. Between her setting up the shop and dealing with Kyle, she hadn't the chance to sit back and think about everything that's happened over the last month.

She absentmindedly searched for the symbol she'd seen on the pocket watch and boxes and read into it. The tea kettle whistled when she got to a page about a rogue faction. As much as she wanted to dig more into it, she was tired from working all day and the drain of having to deal with Kyle.

"I am not a drain."

"I swear to all that's holy, Kyle, if you don't leave my bedroom this minute, I will do whatever I need to in order to make sure you disappear permanently." Alice didn't even glance at the dumbwaiter where she knew Kyle stood.

"Fine. Fine."

Alice knew Kyle had left; he'd been nothing but polite for the most part.

She debated opening the dumbwaiter the next morning to make sure the boxes were still inside, but if they weren't, there was nothing she could do about it.

Not seeing anything out of place, she left to run her errands.

Hoping to find a hair stylist who could work with her curly hair, she pulled up to the first salon she found and went inside.

"Do you take walk-ins?" she asked as the bell over the door jingled, and two women looked up.

"We do. What would you like done?"

"I want to refresh my look for the grand opening of my store tomorrow."

"What store do you own?"

"I own an antiques store downtown. It's right next to Old Stone Architectural Preservation."

"Sweet Scoops is gone?" The younger of the two ladies was wiping down her station.

"No, I'm on the other side."

"You're in Morgan's place. How is it?" The older woman sat Alice in the chair.

"Cluttered, but I'm getting it organized."

"No bumps in the night or voices?"

"No, why?" Alice played dumb.

"The place is rumored to be full of ghosts."

Alice laughed. "I haven't heard anything, and the price was great."

"I get it, and you'll have a lot of foot traffic."

"I'm hoping. Especially since I moved here from Oregon to open it."

The younger woman, having finished cleaning, sat next to Alice. "Have you met the owner of Old Stone yet?"

"No, I haven't seen anyone go in or out of the building yet, but I've been busy trying to get the store ready to open."

The two women looked at each other before laughing.

Alice looked up. "What?"

"Oh, nothing. The owner can be a bit …." The younger woman gave the older one a pleading look for help.

"Stand-offish, aggressive, passive aggressive, stubborn, snotty, snarky." As the woman took a breath, Alice held up her hand, stopping her.

"I get the point. Hopefully, I hope I don't cross their path anytime soon. I can't deal with people like that with everything else going on."

"Hun, you'll know it when you meet 'em." The older woman laughed as she cut Alice's hair.

"I appreciate the heads up. I'm already dealing with this guy who thinks I have something of his, yet either doesn't know or won't tell me what it is. Heck, I barely know what half the stuff in the store even is."

"Let me guess. Short, fat guy with an attitude?" The older woman continued the conversation as the younger woman approached the front counter to help another client.

"How did you know?"

"He harassed Kyle more times than not."

"You knew Kyle?"

"I did. I went out to dinner with him a few times after his wife died. Nothing romantic. His wife, Delores, and I were good friends. After she died, I tried to be a friend."

"I understand. There were a lot of people who were good friends to me after my husband died."

"I'm sorry to hear. I'm done with your hair. Did you want anything else?"

Alice assessed her hair in the mirror. "No, this is perfect. I didn't catch your name. I'm Alice Tidway."

"I'm Wendy, and I hope to see you again soon."

"You will. This is fantastic. Please come by the store tomorrow. It's the grand opening."

"I'm here all day tomorrow, but I should be able to get down there during my lunch. Especially since I own the place."

Alice thanked her and waved on her way out the door. Admiring herself in the mirror, she fluffed up her hair. It was perfect. As she got into her car, she saw a black car creep by.

Shaking off the weird feeling she had, she finished her errands and grabbed something to eat before going back to her house. She sat on the couch and felt the urge to look out her window from her bedroom overlooking the backside of the building.

A similar black car drove by. She couldn't be sure it was the same one from the parking lot, but she felt a sense of worry creep up her back.

"Kyle?"

"Yes?" He appeared next to her.

"I have a feeling I may have been followed by a black car. It drove by, but can you watch for it while I eat and read some?"

"Sure, if it comes back, what do you want me to do?"

"I don't know. I'm probably being paranoid."

"Isn't paranoia a symptom of menopause?" Kyle asked.

"No, not that I've heard of. Can you please just watch?"

"Of course. Don't worry. If anything is amiss, I'll let you know." Kyle disappeared before Alice could thank him.

He didn't come back the entire night.

She dreamed of a black car with teeth chasing her down an alley. The alley stretched on and on, with no doors or side streets to escape down. The car was about to hit her as she woke with a start. Looking at the clock, she realized it was already six in the morning, so there was no point in trying to fall back to sleep.

Chapter Six

Alice took a step back and regarded her new sign she'd hired a young woman named Katie to create for the front window. Katie had done a fantastic job of creating a welcoming sign. She was a window artist, and Alice would definitely have her create new windows for each holiday.

She had an hour before opening, so she went upstairs to get a fresh cup of tea quickly before finishing her breakfast she'd left sitting on the counter. She hadn't seen Kyle all morning. While not specifically worried, he always seemed to be around when she was doing stuff with the store, but not this time.

Waiting to unlock the door, she heard a knock from the front. She opened the shades to see Tara and a young man.

"What are you doing here?" Alice hugged Tara.

"We thought we would drive down to help. Mom, this is Ty." Tara motioned to the man standing next to her.

"Pleasure meeting you, ma'am." Ty and Alice shook hands.

"Nice to meet you. This is a wonderful surprise. We have about ten minutes before I need to open. Do you want a quick tour?"

"Ty is going to visit his family. He's from Palm Coast, which isn't far south of here. He'll come back tomorrow … if it's okay for me to stay the night?"

"Of course it is. The guest bedroom is still a bedroom. Thanks for driving, Ty. I hope you have a good time with your family." Alice smiled and Tara hugged him before he left.

"What do you need to me to do?" Tara asked after Ty left the store.

"Let's get the shade and blinds up and unlock the door. Having you here will be great because I can mingle with customers while you run the cash register. Sound good??"

"Sounds good to me." Tara and Alice went to work getting the place open. From the time they opened the door, there was a steady flow of traffic.

For the next two hours, Alice and Tara were busy running back and forth to the back, grabbing more stuff and making sales.

Alice still hadn't seen Kyle and was surprised he wasn't around.

"Why don't you take lunch while I run everything out here?" Alice asked Tara after a solid three hours of traffic and business.

"I can do that. You have food upstairs?"

"I do; I have leftovers and enough fixings for whatever you want."

"Fine, I'll go eat and bring you something when I'm done." Tara hugged her mom before going upstairs.

With people browsing but no one nearby, Alice snuck into the office. "Kyle, are you around?"

There was no response, but she saw someone approaching the counter with a lamp, so she went to help her customer.

"Thank you for coming in. Did you find everything you were looking for?" Alice rang up the lamp.

"Yes, it's wonderful having this place open again. I used to come here all the time growing up, and there was always something interesting to find." The elderly man smiled at Alice.

"I'm glad." Alice took the man's money and gave him change. "I hope to see you again soon."

"You absolutely will."

The man smiled on his way out the door.

Alice watched him walk out as Wendy came in.

Coming out from behind the counter, Alice greeted Wendy. "How are you today?"

"I'm great. Finally got a minute to breathe. I don't know if it's the weather or what, but everyone seems to want their hair cut or colored this weekend."

"I bet it beats the slow times."

"It does. I like what you've done with the place. It's brighter in here than it used to be."

"Thank you. I installed some new lighting and changed out the window coverings. Are you looking for something specific, or are you coming to browse?"

"I never know when I come in here. For right now, attend to your other customers, and we'll catch up later."

Alice smiled at the two people standing at the counter, ready to check out. She hadn't expected her first day open to be this busy, but she was happy about it. It was something new, and as time passed, fewer people would come in, which was to be expected.

"You know, I initially came in to see how the place was after Old Man Morgan died, but I found this picture, and I had to have it," Alice overheard the lady standing in line tell her friend as she passed them on her way to the counter.

After checking both people out, Alice saw she still had another four hours left, and she needed to restock while there was a lull in customers. If it kept up like this, she would need to go to estate sales much sooner than she'd expected.

It'll refill itself. Don't worry, Kyle's voice was muted.

Alice didn't see Kyle wherever he was hiding. "Where have you been?"

You miss me already? His voice was clearer this time.

Alice turned to face him while answering, "No, but you've been a pain in my butt this whole time, so I didn't think you'd miss this."

"I was down in the basement. I heard your daughter's here helping."

"She is, and what were you doing in the basement?"

"Looking at stuff. Speaking of which, you should probably start bringing out more antiques." Kyle motioned to the two people who had left empty-handed.

"I will when Tara comes back downstairs after her lunch."

"Who are you talking to, Mom?" Tara stood behind her with a sandwich.

"Myself. I need to bring more stuff to the front. It's getting to be slim pickings out there."

"Why don't you eat, and I'll handle it. Anything specific you want from the back?"

Alice didn't know the answer, but a customer was ready to check out before she could think more about it.

"Just tell her to grab whatever's at the front and work her way backwards."

"Tara, please grab whatever is closest, and work backwards from there."

"Weird way of organizing but will do." Tara placed her mom's sandwich and plate on the counter before she took over so Alice could step away to the back briefly.

"Will it work for her?" Alice's voice was quiet.

"She's your kid, so it should. If not, we can rearrange it later."

"Who is this 'we'? You got a mouse in your pocket?" Alice asked as another customer came up.

"You working through lunch?" The customer placed the metal toy car on the counter.

"Since this is the first weekend, yes. Hopefully, I'll hire someone to help me soon."

"Good help is hard to find. I should know. I own Sweet Scoops, the ice cream store on the other side of Old Stone's."

"Nice to meet you. I've been meaning to come down and get some ice cream, but I've been so busy getting this place up and ready to reopen."

The guy chuckled. "I completely understand. Thankfully, my wife is watching the store long enough for me to come down and check things out. I didn't expect to find this toy car. I had one just like it when I was a kid, so I'm going to display it in the store."

Pulling the receipt from the feeder, Alice handed it to him. "Thank you, and I'll try to get down there later today. You're open after five, right?"

"Usually until eight — unless it's really busy. Then whenever we stop getting customers. We try to make as much money as we can during the busy season. Thanks again. I look forward to seeing you around." The man took his toy car and left.

Alice was eating as Tara came out with a heap of new merchandise in her arms. "The back is a mess. I don't know how you know where anything is. The back wall is nothing but boxes full of random antiques."

"I know. It seems like every day there's something new I haven't sorted yet." Alice laughed, knowing it was the truth, but Tara didn't.

"She seems like a good kid." Kyle watched Tara go back to get another armload of antiques.

"She really is. Tara was already out of the house when her dad died. It was rough on her, but we're working through it together."

"When my Delores died, my kids were all grown, and even my grandkids were adults by then."

"Did she know you could talk to ghosts?"

"She did. I didn't tell her in the beginning because I figured she'd think I was crazy."

Processing the next customer's payment, she considered Kyle's words. It was funny; two people from different generations and different families had the same idea.

"Ten minutes until we close," Alice called out to the remaining customers.

While they lined up, she glanced outside and thought she saw the black car from before. Shaking her head, she finished up the customers and followed the last one out. She thanked them for coming in, locked the door, and closed the shade and blinds. A quick check of the front showed most of the morning's items were gone, suggesting they'd been sold.

"You want to go get dinner, Mom?"

"Sure. Let's get some ice cream from Sweet Scoops — the place down the street after dinner. The owner came in earlier and bought a toy car for the shop. I've been meaning to try it since I bought the store."

"Sounds good. Let me run upstairs and grab my purse so we can go."

Tara went upstairs, so Alice called for Kyle. "Did you see the black car drive by earlier?"

"No, I was paying more attention to the customers. Sorry. Do you want me to keep an eye out while you're at dinner?"

"It would be great if you could. We shouldn't be gone long because we still need to restock the front when we get back."

"Mom? Are you ready?"

"I am. How long can you stay tomorrow?"

"Ty's picking me up at around five so we can get back before it gets dark. Alright?"

"Absolutely. If it's this busy tomorrow, I might need to hire someone to help. I don't know if I'll have time to run back and forth to get more merchandise with so many customers in the store."

"You could close for an hour during lunch to restock and eat. You need to remember to eat."

"I can't imagine it'll be this busy all the time." Alice thought about it as they entered the Sunset Grille. Sitting at their table, they ordered their food and talked about Tara's work.

"I can't believe how much you have in the back. Every time I went back there, I discovered something new."

"You should see the basement. If you thought the back was bad, the basement is ten times worse."

"There's a basement?" Tara asked between eating fries.

"There is, and the upstairs, as you saw, is fantastic. Oh, and there's a dumbwaiter to help bring items up from the basement, too. There's also a car downstairs."

Tara dropped her fry. "How did the realtor not know about any of this? Or do you think they knew and didn't tell us?"

"Who knows? It would have increased the price they could have asked for it." Alice was thinking the same thing. How did the realtor not know about so many things, and why did they ask so little?

"It makes no sense. Hey, Mom?" Tara started again.

"Yeah?"

"Have you noticed a black car following us, or at least driving around us a lot?"

Alice had hoped Tara wouldn't see the car, but since she had, Alice debated what to tell her.

"I have. Do you think I should call the cops? There are probably hundreds of black cars in St. Augustine, if not thousands."

Tara mulled it over for a few seconds. "True, but it seems odd, you know?"

"If we see it again tomorrow, I'll give the police a call. Please try to find a license plate or something so I can tell them anything other than just 'it's a black car'?" Alice didn't want to worry her, but this was the second day in a row she'd seen it. With Trent and Alistair showing up before the store had opened, Alice was feeling somewhat paranoid.

"Are you ready for ice cream?" Tara paid the bill.

"You didn't have to pay; I could have taken care of it."

"It's fine. You can buy the ice cream." Tara led the way out of the restaurant, with Alice close behind.

"Why do I think we're going to spend more on ice cream than we did on dinner?" Alice commented right before they opened the door to Sweet Scoops. Alice really enjoyed the closeness of the buildings versus in Oregon, where she had to drive everywhere.

"Because we have to stock up, and I want to take some back with me to the base." Tara laughed as she went into the store.

Rolling her eyes, Alice followed.

The store was bright and cheery with balloons and ice cream themed signs. On the counter rested the toy car the owner had purchased earlier, with small flower arrangements on each side. It fit right in like it had always been there.

Alice made a mental note to give the store first choice if anything ice cream related came in.

"Hey, Alice. How did your first day go?"

"Good! It was super busy. Thanks for asking. What's good?" Alice smiled as she reviewed the menu full of assorted flavors.

"Everything is homemade, and if you don't like any of these flavors, we have a few super-secret ones in the back." He winked as he went to help the next person in line.

"These all sound so good. How big is your freezer?" Tara laughed as she went down the line.

"Not big enough for the eyes you're giving that ice cream. I think I'll start with two and come back later for more. It isn't like I'm moving anytime soon."

"True. Let me call Ty and see if he wants anything. He'll have to wait until tomorrow, but with the way this shop smells, I think it'll be hard not to eat his, too."

"I'm sure you'll manage." Alice saw Tara go through her contacts and find Ty's number before going outside to call him.

Watching the line shorten, Alice decided on the two flavors she would start with. A Toasted Marshmallow Hot Cocoa and Chocolate Mint Explosion.

Right before it was her turn, Tara returned.

"How's Ty?"

"He's good. Told me to get him something with pecan in it. Do you know what you want?"

"I do. I saw two pecan types, so you should probably hurry up with making your decision."

Tara ambled up and down the freezer cabinet one more time before coming up right as Alice was placing her order.

"I would like butter pecan and coconut chia, please."

"Sounds tasty. Can I try the coconut? He can keep the butter pecan." Alice paid the bill, and they sat to wait.

"For tomorrow, do you want me to do the same thing I did today?"

"I don't know. What do you think?" Alice drummed her fingers on the table.

"I think you should be the one talking to people and running back and forth. Put a face to the business."

"I guess I can run around and help people and bring more merchandise to the front."

"My feet thank you." Tara grimaced as she moved.

Alice thanked the girl who brought their ice cream.

"Do you want to eat them here or go back to the house?"

"And let the extra ice cream melt? Absolutely not. Let's go back and watch a random comedy movie." Tara stood with her two ice cream containers.

"That sounds like a great idea." Alice waved to the owner before picking up her containers.

He waved back before helping another customer. The place was as busy as her store had been earlier in the day.

Alice paused, reading all the signs taking up the one entire wall.

Leaving the shop, she turned to see Tara reaching the antiques store. Tara opened the door, and Alice saw a black car turn onto the street they were on.

She couldn't see who was in the car, but when they saw her, they sped up in her direction.

Jumping back into the doorway of Sweet Scoops, the car rushed by. Alice was able to take a picture of the license plate right before it took a left at the end of the street.

Shaking, Alice got back onto the sidewalk and rushed to the antiques store. Her eyes were focused on the ground, and about halfway there, she bumped into someone.

"I'm so sorry." Alice glanced up at the shorter woman, who was glaring at her. Standing next to her was a tall figure wearing a blue cloak covering their entire body.

"Watch where you're going next time, geez," the woman growled at her.

"Again, I'm sorry," Alice squeaked as she stepped around them and made for the antiques store's door. Stepping toward the door, she looked back at the two, still standing in the same place and seeming to have a discussion. Before they could catch her staring, she went inside, realizing Tara probably was already upstairs.

"Kyle?"

"Did you get me ice cream, too?"

"No, I didn't. Since you know you can't eat it."

"You could still buy my favorite, and you could eat it."

Alice rolled her eyes. "What's your favorite?"

"French Vanilla."

"So boring. You could've said Peppermint Patty, or even Moose Tracks."

"It's not boring when you put sprinkles, fudge, and butterscotch on it."

"I'm a purest. Only straight ice cream for me."

"Now who's the boring one? Anyway, why did you call for me? Your daughter is flipping through streaming services, trying to find the corniest comedies."

"I was almost hit by the black car; can you keep an eye out for it? I think whoever's driving is getting braver, and I'm going to call the cops in the morning."

"Will do. Enjoy your evening." Kyle disappeared before Alice joined Tara upstairs, putting one of her containers into the freezer. She wasn't paying attention to which one, so grabbing a spoon she knew it would be a surprise.

Nathan would buy ice cream and not let her know the flavors. He would surprise her with a bowl, and she'd had to guess what it was.

She smiled as she joined Tara on the couch.

"Find a movie?"

"I think we're going to watch Dear Santa."

"Is it a comedy?"

"It's got excellent reviews, and it has Jack Black."

"But it isn't Christmas. Are you sure you want to watch a Christmas movie?" Alice cocked her head.

Tara wasn't a huge Christmas fan, always liking Halloween much more.

"Yeah, let's do it." Tara turned on the movie she'd paused.

Alice and Tara settled back to watch the movie while eating their ice cream. Alice didn't want to worry Tara even though, in the back of her mind, she was worried.

After the first movie, Tara wasn't ready for bed, so she suggested a second movie. Right before she clicked play, Alice saw Kyle waving at her from next to the TV. After making sure Tara didn't see him, she excused herself.

"What's going on?"

"Sorry I came up without asking or being invited, but I wanted to let you know the car drove by again just now."

"Same license plate?" Alice pulled up the photo from her phone and showed Kyle.

"Exactly the same. Before you ask, no, I didn't see who was driving."

"Thanks anyway. I'm going to watch another movie. Anything else happens, let me know immediately."

"Will do." Kyle disappeared, and Alice went back into the living room.

Tara was on the phone, and when she saw Alice, she quickly ended the call.

"Ready for the next movie?"

"Yup, let me get a cup of tea to have with the rest of this ice cream. Do you want a cup of tea or coffee?"

"Coffee would be great. Thank you."

"Was Ty on the phone?" Alice pulled the two cups out and set the kettle on the stove to boil. Turning on the coffeemaker to brew, she turned for her answer.

"Yeah, he made it back to his parent's place after dinner. Is it still alright with you if he picks me up around five tomorrow?"

"Sure. I think after we close tomorrow, I'm going to take a long bath and worry about cleaning up everything downstairs on Monday when we're closed."

"Sounds like a plan. You ready?"

"Absolutely."

Alice and Tara watched another movie with no issues.

When the movie was over, Alice let Tara know she was going to bed. "I don't know about you, but I'm wiped out. I'm going to shower and go to bed, then we can get up and do it all again in the morning."

"Sounds like a plan. I think I'll get ready for bed, too. Have a good night, Mom."

"You too." Alice hugged Tara before each went to their rooms.

Alice reconsidered her decision to turn the guest bedroom into an office as she had planned. It was nice having Tara around, even if it was only for a weekend at a time.

Going to sleep, Alice was tired but happy.

Chapter Seven

Alice awoke early the next morning to the sound of clanging in the kitchen. Throwing on a robe, she found Tara cooking in the kitchen.

"You don't cook."

"I've started cooking. It helps me stay healthy."

"What did you make?"

"Omelets and coffee. I would've added fruit if you'd had any." Tara placed the plates on the table before going back to get the coffee.

"Thank you. I haven't had the chance to get fresh fruit."

"I didn't make tea, but I made coffee, and I know you'll drink it."

"If I have, to I'll drink it. How much coffee do you drink a day?"

Tara laughed at her mother as she placed the two cups of coffee on the table.

"Only about a pot a day, not counting the energy drinks."

"Wow, how much caffeine can you ingest before you get sick? That doesn't sound healthy. Maybe *I* should be the one talking to *your* doctor instead of the other way around."

Tara shrugged. "With how some of my younger seamen are, I need all the caffeine I can get."

"This is good, thank you. Do you have problems with them sometimes?"

"Nothing I can't handle. You know how people can be." Tara rolled her eyes.

"You need to get dressed so we can get downstairs. We open in —" Alice glance at her watch "—an hour, I have to get ready." She looked at the plates.

"Mom, I've got them. You go get ready." Tara picked up the plates to put them into the dishwasher.

***

"Ready?"

"Let's do it."

At the bottom of the stairs, Alice watched for Kyle but didn't see him.

"Do you want me to bring some stuff in while you open the doors?" Tara set her coffee on the counter.

Not responding, Alice opened the blinds and the door shade.

There were already four people standing in line outside the door.

Smiling, she unlocked the door.

"Welcome. Please come in and look around. We're restocking at the moment, so please excuse any misplaced items."

They smiled as they entered the store.

Alice passed Tara, whose arms were full of stock to be put out. By the time she got back to the counter, there was already a customer ready to check out.

It was shaping up to be another busy day. Alice definitely needed to hire someone to help her because there was no way she could run the business by herself.

They worked solid until lunchtime, when Tara took over for Alice so she could eat. Alice made enough soup and sandwiches for both of them. Carrying it downstairs, she placed it on the counter.

"If you want to stay here, I'll start bringing more from the back," Alice told Tara.

"Just so you know, something weird is going on back there. I can't get through it fast enough." Tara lifted her spoon, about to dig in.

"Maybe the previous owner had someone drop some things off? I haven't gotten through all the documents in the office, so there's a chance there's something in there about pending deliveries being made."

"In that case, make sure you keep records. You don't want to have to pay for something they didn't drop off."

Kyle popped up near Tara. "You know why merchandise is appearing."

She couldn't respond but answered Tara, "I'm sure there's an inventory somewhere. Perhaps I should bring some stuff up from the basement instead of the stockroom."

"We haven't brought anything up from there yet. I'll call you if I need you." Tara waved Alice off as customers came up.

Going down into the basement, Alice searched for things she could bring upstairs to the store. She found a basket to carry it in after some digging around. The basket was full in no time, and she hauled it upstairs.

"This is some cool stuff. I wonder why it was all downstairs." Tara picked through the basket.

"Good, you can put it out." Alice handed it over for Tara to stock.

Tara started her work up front while Alice cataloged the customer's selections.

"Mom?"

Alice lifted her eyes from the register and saw Tara holding the door open for a young uniformed police officer. Chiding herself internally for forgetting to call the police about the car, Alice stood a little straighter.

"Hi, I'm Alice Tidway. How can I help you?"

"One of your neighbors reported they've seen a black sedan driving up and down the road repeatedly over the last couple of days. I wanted to check with you and see if you'd noticed anything suspicious."

"Actually, Mom, we did see that black car, remember?" Tara volunteered before Alice raised her hand.

"Can we talk in the back? Tara, are you good up here without me for a minute?"

"Absolutely. Ty should be here soon, so he can help if needed."

"If you wouldn't mind following me, Officer?"

She took him to the stockroom because the office wasn't ready to meet anyone in yet. When she got to the back, she looked around.

Tara was right, the place was vomiting up antiques. She realized it was just as big of a mess as the office.

"Officer?"

"Rivera, ma'am."

"Thank you, Officer Rivera. Yes, I noticed a black sedan a couple of times. In fact, yesterday I was on my way back from Sweet Scoops when I think it tried to hit me. I can't be sure, but it sped up once it saw me. It drove past just as I got into the doorway of my store. I got the license plate if you need it."

"It would be appreciated. Can I get your name and phone number so I can add it to the report?"

"Do you really think there's something suspicious going on?"

"I doubt it, but it's always good to double check. Then, if any property damage or theft occurs that could be connected to this vehicle, there will be a report we can refer to. It's always good to document things like this."

Alice considered what he'd said. "Good point. Thank you, Officer Rivera." She gave him the information he requested and texted the photo of the license plate.

She followed him out to the counter, where he saw a small jewelry box sitting at the bottom of the basket.

"I'm not supposed to be buying stuff, but this looks just like the jewelry box my mom had when I was growing up. Can I buy it?"

Tara looked from the item to the basket. "I thought I'd put everything out already. Of course you can." She told the officer the price, he paid, and left smiling.

"Strange. I know it was empty when I brought it back up here."

"It was small. You probably just missed it."

Tara glanced around, making sure no one else could hear her. "You're probably right. There is something off about this place."

"All old buildings have something off about them. I wouldn't be surprised if all the buildings in St. Augustine have a history of someone dying in them."

"True. I guess I'm just not used to it yet." Tara's focus was diverted to a customer who was having trouble pulling something down from a shelf. "Just a minute, ma'am. I can help you."

Alice lingered on their conversation.

I wonder why I haven't seen any ghosts other than Kyle and Alistair.

"Because not all people stay, and not all ghosts want to be seen." Kyle materialized in front of her. The more he did it, the less she jumped.

She believed Kyle, but it made her wonder how many ghosts could be hanging out in the antiques store.

"There's a few, but they're nice, and they don't want to bother you."

"Oh great, so if you ever leave, I could end up with another you? And didn't I tell you no reading my mind?"

"Sorry about that. I'm not used to people being able to see or hear me. I'm not going anywhere. You're stuck with me. Someone has to show you the ropes of the ghost world."

Alice rolled her eyes as a steady flow of customers wanted to check out. She felt his presence leave and was still surprised he didn't want to watch all the customers coming and going.

"Ten minutes until we close. Please start making your way to the register for checkout," Alice heard Tara call out as she saw Ty walk through the door.

Tara's face brightened. In between helping people, Tara and Ty chatted.

Once the last person was gone, Tara locked the door behind them, and Ty followed her to the counter.

"Another busy day, Mom."

"Yeah, it was, but I have tomorrow and Tuesday to get ready for the rest of the week. You need to leave soon, right?"

Checking her phone, Tara agreed. "Let me get my stuff. I have your ice cream, too."

"Good, I'm looking forward to it. When I was a kid, my parents brought me here for ice cream, but it was called something else. Same location, though."

"While Tara's upstairs, why don't you look around a little? You haven't been here long enough to see everything," Alice offered as Tara jogged upstairs to get her stuff.

"Thank you. I will. I think I've been in here before, but I don't remember when."

"Is your family from Palm Coast?"

"Some of them. We don't talk to all of them, so I don't know where some of the extended family is from. I know I was born in Palm Coast."

"It must be nice to be stationed so close to home." Alice smiled as Ty picked up a small spoon.

"Bringing Tara up here gives me an excuse to see them, which they're pretty happy about. I really didn't visit them much until you moved here."

"I'm ready." Tara set the ice cream on the counter.

"Have a safe drive, and please call me when you get to the base." Alice hugged Tara.

"Absolutely. We might stop and have dinner, but more than likely, I'll drive while he eats the ice cream before it melts."

Ty was already reaching for it. Tara laughed as he pulled his hand away like a kid who had gotten caught sneaking into the cookie jar.

"I'll take you to dinner. It's the least I can do for you paying for gas. I even brought a cooler for my ice cream." Ty offered his hand to Alice.

Shaking it, she smiled. "I hope to see you again."

Tara waved as Alice followed her and Ty out the door.

Alice stepped out and looked both ways before returning to the store and locking the door. Lowering the shade and turning the blinds, she leaned against the door, taking a deep breath and closing her eyes.

"This weekend was a busy two days." Kyle shimmered into view on Alice's left.

"Yes, it was. Were you here when the police officer came by?"

"Technically, I was here, but I was playing rummy in the basement with a couple of the blue-hairs. They're a bunch of card sharks."

"Do you mean older women 'blue-hairs', or younger people with hair dyed blue?"

"Older woman, like my age. Why would anyone voluntarily dye their hair blue?" Kyle stepped back as if he was shocked.

"Don't be like that. I'm sure you had customers with dyed hair. You didn't die all that long ago."

"True, but never blue. Other colors, yes, and my Delores would dye her hair to get rid of the grays until I finally convinced her gray hair was beautiful." Kyle smiled as he remembered his wife.

"How long ago did she pass?"

"15 years ago."

"I'm sorry. It must have been hard living those 14 years without her. Have you ever seen her?"

"No. I'd hoped to, but the minute she died, the reaper came and retrieved her, and she left. She led a good life and had nothing she needed to finish."

"Wait, reaper?"

"You don't think Death does everything himself? No. In fact, he has a bunch of reapers in this area. They don't call Florida 'Death's waiting room' for no reason."

"I thought the phrase was 'God's waiting room'? Either way, I guess I never really thought about it. Even when Nathan was sick and dying, I didn't think about reapers, death, or even the afterlife. Is there an afterlife?"

"Yeah, but I don't know what it is. I asked Death a time or two, but he never answered, so I figured he either didn't know or didn't want to tell me."

"I wonder why? Back to the subject of the police officer since you were playing games downstairs. The black car that's been driving around? Someone else called it in, so Officer Rivera came to talk to me about it."

"You give him the license plate number?"

"Of course, but I have a feeling I know who's behind the wheel, or possibly in the back seat."

"Who?"

"Trent. I think he's been stalking me and trying to get whatever he's been looking for. Speaking of men I don't particularly want to see, we haven't had a visit from our ghost lately, either."

Kyle laughed. "Oh, he's *our* ghost now? What am I, then?"

Alice thought about it for a second. "You're *my* ghost. Think about it. Can anyone else see you? If not, then you're *my* ghost. He's *our* ghost because we can both see him."

"A pretty young woman calling me hers. I've had worse." Kyle strutted off toward the counter, head held up with pride.

Alice reconsidered calling him her ghost. She knew it was unlikely she had a tumor, but what if this was all just a midlife crisis or something to do with menopause? She didn't recall seeing anything about auditory or visual hallucinations in her readings about perimenopause, but everyone was different, right?

"Since the store isn't open tomorrow, I think I'm going to go upstairs, have dinner, and relax."

"You're not planning on being open seven days a week?" Kyle gaped.

"Not to begin with. I need to find staff before I can even consider it. I bought this to enjoy my middle age, not be stuck behind a counter 56 hours a week. It's too much for one person."

"Makes sense. I used to have days off, but once the family moved away and Delores died, I didn't have much to do other than run the store."

"For right now, I want to enjoy the beach, maybe shop once in a while, travel."

"You'll need to find someone you can trust."

"Already working on it." Alice already knew who she wanted to hire. She still needed to talk to Francis to make sure she had the reserves to pay an employee for at least six months in case business dropped, which Alice knew was a likely possibility. Nowhere was this busy every day, except maybe Sweet Scoops, and they probably slowed down during certain months.

"Hey Kyle, when does the off-season happen here?" Might as well make him useful since he would be hanging around for a while, according to him.

"Usually, August through October, but still not slow-slow, and it's mainly only slow then because it's the busiest part of hurricane season and the hottest months of the year. Locals usually come in then."

"We're in the second week of April. It gets busier than this?" Without a doubt, Alice was going to have to hire someone, and fast, if tourism picked up more than this.

"There will be some days where the people are so thick during Nights of Lights, you can't see the road in front of the building because it's constant foot traffic. The city will close some of the roads to vehicles because there are so many people."

Alice was calculating how much she'd made in the last two days versus what a 'busy' day could mean. She could be open three days a week and pay off the building in less than a year. Something to think about tomorrow when she called Francis to discuss hiring someone. In the meantime, there was a frozen dinner with her name on it, along with a bath and a glass of wine.

"I'm off work for the rest of the night. Tomorrow, I can pick up in the office and get more organized."

"Our weekly Sunday bridge game starts in the backroom soon. If you need anything, yell for me." Kyle waved as he faded away.

His calendar is fuller than mine.

Alice debated eating the frozen dinner or ordering something. With how much she'd made over the last two days, she could afford to treat herself.

Sitting at the table in her apartment, she searched for an online delivery place and scrolled through their options. Chinese sounded great, so she ordered her favorite dish and waited until the driver said they were nearby.

Thirty minutes later, the driver texted they were out front, so Alice grabbed the tip she'd planned to give them and unlocked the front door. A young man stood on the front step with her food.

She smiled and gave him the tip in exchange for the food. When left to go back to his vehicle, Alice saw Alistair standing across the road, glaring at her.

Quickly closing and locking the door, she rushed upstairs. She considered calling Kyle but didn't want to bother him.

Maybe locking the door would stop Alistair from coming in. She knew he'd lied about where he was from. What else had he lied about?

While she tried to relax, she was worried about Alistair appearing out of the middle of the floor or something for the rest of the night. Having a glass of wine in the bathtub helped, but she had locked the door just in case.

They're ghosts. A locked door won't do anything to stop them from coming in.

With St. Augustine being as old as it was, there was probably an occult store or something to help with her ghost problem. She didn't want to block them all because she liked Kyle being around, but she wouldn't mind there were certain rooms they couldn't come into, like the bathroom.

Boiling the water for her tea, Alice made a list of what she needed to do the following day. Alice had always been a list maker.

When Nathan got sick and died, she'd made lists of what needed to be done. When she was planning the funeral with the help of her friends and family, she still made lists to keep from forgetting anything. It wasn't menopause or her getting older causing the list making; she'd always done it. It settled her mind and allowed her to think about other things versus getting anxious about forgetting to do something.

Tara would tease her about it when she was younger, but Alice had caught Tara making her own lists several times, especially right before she went to college and joined the military.

The rest of the night was quiet. There were a couple times she swore she heard Kyle laughing downstairs, but when she listened harder, it was quiet. Not thinking about Alistair, Trent, or any work stuff, she fell into a deep sleep, aided by the bath and wine.

Chapter Eight

By nature, Alice was not a morning person. Frequently during her life, she was forced to wake up early, but when she could sleep in, she thoroughly enjoyed it.

Lying in bed, she thought about adjusting the store hours. Depending on how the next month went, maybe the hours should be 11-7 instead of the unwritten 9-5 she had now. She thought about the change as she got up and made herself brunch.

She realized Tara had never let her know if she'd made it home. A spike of panic shot through her as Alice texted Tara, knowing she was most likely already at work.

Hey! Didn't hear from you last night. Hope you made it back to the base safely. Love you.

Putting her phone down, since a watched phone never dings, she went to get ready. She needed to call Francis. Even though Francis was her accountant, she liked to keep track of the smaller scale finances on her own. She paid him well to keep track of the larger ones.

Working on getting the office organized was also of high importance. If there was time later, Alice wanted to explore the town again. Before anything, she wanted to make sure Alistair hadn't snuck inside last night.

"Kyle?" It was weird calling for a ghost, and she was worried she was keeping him at her beck and call.

"Yes?" He appeared near the fridge.

"Are you okay with me randomly calling you? I understand you might not have much to do, but I feel weird calling you when I need you."

"You need me?" Kyle put his hands under his chin and rapidly blinked flirtatiously.

"Stop. You know what I mean."

"I do and I don't mind. Most of the time, I'm in a sort of limbo, but not *the* limbo, if you know what I mean. Here but not here. I can come and go as I please, but when nothing is going on, I watch the world like a TV show. When you call, I come out of it."

"You're okay with it?"

"I have literally nothing better to do. It isn't like I can spend all night organizing for you. Speaking of which, the stockroom is a mess."

"You don't say." Alice shook her head. She knew it was a mess but didn't know how to clean it since things randomly appeared whenever and wherever they wanted to.

"What did you need?" Kyle stuck his head into the fridge.

"Did Alistair sneak into the shop last night?"

"I didn't see him, and the entire group was here, so if anyone did, they would've noticed. No one mentioned anyone showing up, though."

"What's the entire group?" Alice was afraid of the answer since it sounded like a ghost orgy had taken place downstairs while she slept.

"There are four rummy players, five musicians, and a couple of artists who come by once in a while."

"You're saying there were at least 12 ghosts hanging out downstairs last night?" Alice couldn't believe her ears, but she was talking to a dead man, so she might need to adjust her beliefs.

"Yeah, the musicians played music. The whole basement was hopping. Didn't see Alistair at all. Maybe he didn't want to make an appearance among the other dead in case someone recognized him?"

"I don't know. I feel he's connected to everything going on, but I can't figure out how."

"I'll ask some of my friends if they've seen anything. Between the rummy players alone, you have over 150 years of history."

"Can you imagine the stories they could tell?" Alice thought out loud.

"I've heard some of their stories, but I don't know if you're going to want to hear them." Kyle chuckled while wiggling his eyebrows.

"Let's put a pin on this conversation. I'm about to call and make sure I have enough money to cover an employee for six months and get some stuff done, so I'll talk to you later."

Kyle nodded and disappeared.

Alice didn't know what to think about a gaggle of ghosts. Was it a gaggle or a herd?

What's the correct plural for a group of ghosts, anyway?

Gaggle was going to have to do until she either thought of something better or found out there was an actual term.

Tara still hadn't replied by the time Alice was ready to call Francis.

While her mom-brain told her she should start calling all the hospitals and police stations between St. Augustine and the base, her adult-woman-brain told her Tara probably forgot, and everything was fine. Alice was hoping her adult brain was right.

Francis picked up on the second ring. "Good morning, afternoon, whatever, Ms. Tidway. How's Florida?"

"Francis, how many times have I told you to call me Alice? You should know better by now." She laughed with him. "Florida is fantastic. I'm actually calling to see if I could swing hiring an employee. Did you get the sales figures from the store for the first two days I emailed you this morning?"

"I saw them when I came in this morning. Very impressive. You know every day won't be this good?"

"Of course, but I was talking to a … fellow business owner, and he said this is one of the slower months, with it picking up for the rest of the year."

"Really? How long do you want to employ the person?"

"Forever? What do you mean?"

"If business slows or stops, how long do you want to ensure the person is employed before you need to think about laying them off? Also, do you know how much you want to pay them?"

"I was thinking 20 an hour because there's some heavy lifting, and the place is a mess. At least 6 months. It would give me time to get everything set up, work out the kinks, and if business slows too much, I could lay them off if I needed to."

Alice could hear the clicking of what sounded like a calculator.

"Even if you take a tenth of what you made over the two days and multiply it by every day you'll be open, you'll have more than enough to pay an employee. You also own the building, so you don't have to worry about a mortgage."

"Thanks. I was thinking along the same lines. I don't like doing anything financial without consulting you."

"Understandable. Also, what do you mean by 'it's a mess'?"

"Francis, let me tell you. The realtor knew nothing about the building. It has a basement, and the back storage room is full — literally to the ceiling. Tara came down over the weekend to help with the grand opening, and even though we spent all weekend moving stuff out of it, I swear it's still as full as it was when I got here."

"Wow. If anyone can organize it, it's you. I saw the money from the credit cards went to your primary account. Did you want me to make a new account and transfer the money into a business account?"

"I didn't think about it. If something happens, I want separation, so please go ahead and do that. You're the best, Francis."

"That's why you pay me the big bucks. I have a meeting I need to get to. If you need anything else, email me, and I'll get to it when I get back."

"Thanks. I don't think I will, but I appreciate it." Alice hung up after Francis said goodbye. It was good having someone financially aware who Alice could trust. It took something off her list of things she needed to worry about. Now, if only Tara would call, text, or even send a carrier pigeon.

Grabbing her purse, she made it downstairs. She'd planned to organize and clean, but after looking at her list, she decided to explore instead. If nothing was accomplished today in the store, Alice could do it tomorrow.

I think having two days closed in a row is the way to go.

Alice pulled her keys out of her purse and opened the door to the basement stairs. Everything seemed to be in the same place as the last time she was down there. Settling into her car, she mentally ran through what she wanted to do.

Alice drove through town. Surprisingly, there weren't many people, so it only took her 20 minutes to fully drive around downtown St. Augustine. As she continued driving, she realized she was heading to the title business.

You know what? Let's see if Cynthia wants a job.

Pulling into the parking lot of the title office, she noticed there was only one car in the lot. Opening the front door, she closed her eyes for a minute to adjust to the lighting before opening them again.

Not seeing anyone in the waiting room other than Cynthia at her desk, Alice greeted her as she stood.

"Did you need something, Ms. Tidway?" Cynthia smiled.

"I came to ask you something. Is Ms. Smalls here? I don't want you to get into trouble."

"No. She had to visit a client to get some documentation needed to close on a property. What can I help you with?"

"Do you enjoy working here?" There was no point not getting straight to the point.

"Not really, but it pays well."

"If you don't mind me asking, how much do you make?"

"I make 15 an hour, and since the minimum wage here is 13 if I didn't want to be in a tipped position, it helps."

"If I could offer you 20 an hour for at least six months, would you be interested?"

"What would I be doing?" Cynthia narrowed her eyes.

"The grand opening of my antiques store was Saturday, and thankfully my daughter came up to help because we were so busy we barely had time to restock. Sunday was the same. If you don't like this job, what do you want to do?"

"I'm an historian. Or at least, I went to school for it. Got my associates, but my mom got sick, and I had to drop out before getting my bachelor's degree."

"Did you want to teach?"

"I would have loved to work in an archive somewhere. Ms. Smalls likes me here; I keep everything organized and readily available for her. But I'm not sure she appreciates me, and this job isn't very fulfilling."

"You don't have to decide right now. I'm closed today and tomorrow, but open at nine on Wednesday. If you're interested, why don't you talk it over with your husband and let me know?"

"Ms. Tidway, why did you say for six months? Is there a time limit to the job?" Cynthia seemed concerned.

"I said it for a few reasons. I was really busy for the first two days, but what if it doesn't stay busy? Could I afford to employ someone essentially forever without making money? I don't know the economy well enough to say it'll be good during the winter, or if the customers drop off. What if the store is damaged by a hurricane? I don't want to give an illusion of more, you understand?"

"Absolutely, and very considerate of you. There is a holiday during the winter months, that the only thing you should concern yourself with is if you can stay open 24 hours straight because it's so busy. It's our busiest time of year. Many business owners I know don't think so far ahead. They either don't hire someone until it's too late, or they hire too many people too early, and either way, it ends up with the business failing."

"Like I said, think about it. I have more running around to do today, but if you're interested, come by tomorrow. I'll be organizing all day, so when the store opens on Wednesday, it'll be all new merchandise."

"Do you have enough inventory to change it up much?"

"You have no idea." Alice laughed. She heard the door behind her open and Ms. Smalls asked Cynthia if there had been any calls, completely ignoring Alice.

"No, Ma'am."

"I didn't realize we had a client. You look familiar. Is there something we can help you with?"

"No, Ms. Smalls. I recently purchased a property and signed the documents with you a few days ago. I stopped by on my way to run errands to see if there was possibly another key. You know how spare keys are always in demand." Alice smiled while trying not to sneer.

"I do remember you. You bought the Morgan property. I don't think we had anything else." Ms. Smalls shifted from Alice to Cynthia.

"Christina, were you able to find anything for her?"

Alice could see Cynthia's jaw clench. "No, ma'am. She was leaving because I couldn't find anything else. Have a good day, ma'am."

Taking the statement as a cue to leave, she waved at Cynthia before nodding to Ms. Smalls on her way out the door.

Alice hoped Cynthia would at least consider working for her. Even if it was only part-time or on the weekends, Alice thought it would help them both a lot.

Sitting in her car, she thought about where to go next. Everything else on her list was store related, but she was feeling restless and wanted to stay out a bit longer.

Snapping her fingers at something she forgot to put on her list, she pulled out her phone. There was still no message from Tara, and Alice was worried. Not worried enough yet to call the police but getting there.

Searching for the shop's name, she put it into GPS and listened for the instructions as she pulled out of the title office's parking lot.

Pulling up in front of Whispers of Wondyr, Alice checked to make sure she was in the right place. The building was brightly painted and looked like one of the many hippy stores in Oregon.

In for a penny.

Alice pushed open the door.

"Hi, welcome to Whispers of Wondyr. I'm Sage. Is there something I can help you with?" A young woman with numerous piercings and tattoos, dark hair, and pale skin greeted her from behind the counter.

"Yes. I've never been in a store like this, and I have a question which could seem really weird."

"Oh, honey. Nothing you can say will sound weird to me."

"Wait until after I tell you to judge."

Alice and Sage laughed.

"I bought a business downtown, and it's older."

"Wait? Did you buy the antiques store?" Sage appeared shocked.

"Yes, how did you know? They're almost all pretty old."

"There aren't many businesses up for sale, so when one goes on the market, everyone knows."

"Oh, I was worried."

"You should be. The place gives me the heebie-jeebies." Sage shuddered.

"Then maybe you were right about my question not being weird. I need something to keep ghosts from coming into a specific area."

"You have ghosts? Tell me more." Sage tapped her fingers together excitedly.

"I'm not saying I have ghosts." Alice cocked an eyebrow. When Sage motioned to keep going, she continued, "I haven't seen a ghost, but if there was a ghost, what could I use to keep them from entering a specific room?" Alice wasn't sure about how much she should tell Sage. She didn't have a bad feeling about her. In fact, she felt at home around her. But she was wary of telling people she saw, or heard, things normally not seen or heard.

"One way is salt. You put it on the doorjamb, but it only stops them from coming into the room through the door. If you're looking for something to cover the entire room, there are a couple of different options. These not ghosts you have, are they good or bad?"

"Ghosts can be bad? I mean, in real life, not in a movie."

Sage turned to a bookcase and pulled a book from the shelf.

"Absolutely, here. I'll let you have this. It's essentially a different version of *The Complete Idiot's Guide to Ghosts.* Obviously, there's more nuanced information not in there, but if nothing else, it'll give you a good starting point."

Alice studied the book and saw the author's name was Sage Wondyr. "Is this you?" Alice showed the cover to Sage.

"Yup, I own this store, have written five books, and speak at conventions around the world."

"Wow, I didn't expect that."

"Was it the tattoos or the piercings?"

"Neither. It was your age, honestly. You're what? 25, at the oldest?"

Sage grinned and brushed her hair back over her shoulder. "You're now my favorite customer. No, I'm 50."

Alice almost dropped the book. "There's *no* way you're older than me. You look so young."

"Coming from a family of witches has some perks. Anyway, back to your nonissue issue. If the presence was evil or negative, you could use sage. Yes, my mom named me after an herb to keep evil at bay. She was a jokester. The problem is, it's short-lived, meaning if you do it on a Friday, and the ghost comes to hang out on the following Monday, they might not have a problem doing so. You would have to continue to apply. Another issue with sage is I only sell ethically sourced sage, which is much more expensive than the stuff you find online."

"You ethically source your sage?" Alice instantly liked this woman and felt Sage would have fit in well in Oregon.

"Yes, I only buy from the local indigenous tribes. They only gather it during certain times. Regardless, I doubt you have the time to do a cleansing ritual every few days. I don't know what your finances look like, but I think what would be best for you is stones."

"Like river rock?"

Laughing, Sage walked out from behind the counter and motioned toward the back of the room.

Alice held on to her new book and followed her back.

"No. Well, yes, like river rock. There are many types of stone. The precious ones like emerald and sapphire, all the way to the more mundane river rock. How big is the room you want to keep everything and anyone out of?"

Alice envisioned how big her bathroom was. "It's about 10X10."

Sage shuffled through some rocks before selecting two. "Here are two I think will help, and I'll grab the other two." She handed them to Alice before skirting around the table and pulling out two more. "Here are the other two. These are clear quartz, smoky quartz, amethyst, and black obsidian. I could explain what each one does, but the book tells you as well. I'll put them in separate bags and label them because this is important. The smoky quartz needs to be on the wall sharing a door and window, if you have one. If not, just the door will work. It creates a barrier like the salt does. The clear quartz needs to be diagonal from the smokey one. Will you be able to remember this, or do I need to write it down?" Sage paused while Alice confirmed she should write it down.

"What about the other two? Where do I put those?"

"I would suggest putting the amethyst closest to where you spend more time. For instance, I have amethyst, albeit a much larger one, near the register because it's where I'm at more than anywhere else. Make sense?"

"Yes, it does. Should I feel … I don't know … something?" Alice didn't have the words, so she motioned uncertainly with her hands.

"Out of your element? In the deep end of the pool? Concerned this is a thing?"

"Yes, all and more." Alice laughed while Sage went back to the counter, laughing as well.

"No, I assume you're not from around here. When you grow up around spirits and the occult, it's part of life. But for someone who moved here recently, it can be a bit jarring. Trust me, you'll be accustomed to all the legends and myths before you know it." Sage rang up the purchases. "Your total is 43.50."

"Wow, it's not as much as I expected it to be. You're charging me for the book, right?" Alice held up the book.

"Yes, because I knew you wouldn't take it for free. Stones aren't always expensive; it's usually the jewelry companies price gouging. Their size contributes to it as well. The quartz I have at my house is worth over 5,000 dollars."

"Wow. I didn't know stones could be so expensive. I didn't realize anything other than gemstones like diamonds were."

Sage brushed away the comment. "Diamonds make up most of the jewelry market."

As she placed Alice's purchases into a paper bag, Alice thought of something.

"I have a question."

"What's up?

"You've called them spirits a few times. I've heard of ghosts, but thought spirits were the same thing. How are they different?"

"This is something not really included in the book because it's advanced for your run-of-the-mill ghost chasers. Many people use them interchangeably to mean the same thing. However, I do not."

“How do you categorize them?”

“Ghosts are visions, remnants of the past. They are usually tied to something, be it a place, event, person, etc. Some say ghosts are on a type of memory loop, so they’ll do the same things over and over.”

“Like in a cemetery or washing dishes?”

“Exactly. To some, a spirit is an entity not tied to a specific time or place but can travel. This is where you get stories of families being followed from house to house. They can usually touch things, move things, and interact with the world. Spirits are also thought to be self-aware enough they can move outside of a ghost’s memory loop.”

“What if they can interact but not move from place to place? Also, what about moving objects like a chair or a book?”

“Ultimately, at the crux of this is that entities which exist after death can be all, none, a bit of both terms. If you want to call them houseguests, call them houseguests.”

“What you're saying is there’s no general consensus, and we’re making it up as we go?”

“Exactly. Now you get it,” Sage confirmed and smiled.

“I have another question. Please feel free to say no, since I’m sure you’re very busy.”

“Hit me with it.” Sage lifted her head as she folded the top of the bag.

“If I get an item which seems occult in nature, or a stone, for instance, could I call you to offer an expert opinion? Obviously, I know you probably don’t know everything about everything occult, but you have access to more options to find out information than I do.”

Sage's eyes lit up. "And to get into Old Man Morgan's building? I'd do it for free."

Alice laughed. "Don't be silly, I'd pay you. You can come by anytime. I'm open Wednesdays through Sundays and will more than likely be organizing and inventorying on Mondays and Tuesdays."

"I haven't been there in years. Let's just say Mr. Morgan and I had a falling out over a crystal ball, and he banned me from the store."

"Well, I'm unbanning you, and if Mr. Morgan happens to drop by, I'll make sure he knows it." Alice winked and left for her car.

So far, she was enjoying St. Augustine and was glad she'd moved. It was time to pick up some food and get back to the store. Checking her phone for missed calls or texts as she turned the key, she called Tara one more time before taking it to the next level.

Tara answered on the first ring. "Hey, Mom."

"Hey, Mom? You didn't message me when you got home, and I've been worried sick all day."

"Sorry. I got back and had an issue with a junior seaman, so I was up all night with her. This morning, I had to go to work, and I'm leaving the office now. Is everything okay?"

"Yes. I was worried since you didn't let me know you'd made it back to base. I know I'm being a mother hen, but still."

"No, I should've messaged you. I'll always be your chicken nugget, and I completely understand why you were worried. I drove the entire way because Ty was too involved with his ice cream. What did you do today?"

"I'm sitting in front of a witchy store, and I offered someone a job."

"Wait, what? A witchy store? Like herbs and stones and candles and stuff?"

"Yeah, it's called Whispers of Wondyr, and it's owned by a nice lady named Sage. I decided if I was going to live in one of … if not *the*… oldest city in the United States, I should probably get some books on the supernatural."

"It makes sense. I never expected you to go into one of those stores. You've always been all about being able to touch something to believe it."

"Well, your mom is growing up. I need to get back to the store and eat. I had breakfast but completely missed lunch. Don't even start. I didn't realize how long I'd been out until I left the witchy store."

"Fine. Drive safe and enjoy your day off. Do you think the person you offered the job to will take it?"

"I have a feeling she will, but I told her to come by tomorrow if she wanted to talk about it. We shall see. Love you."

"Love you, too. Have a good night. I need to get some sleep." Tara sounded tired.

Alice wasn't surprised when Tara got off the phone so fast. She was glad her daughter was okay. Raising a kid until they were adults didn't make the protective feelings go away. In fact, sometimes it made the feelings worse, especially when said daughter moved across the country not once, but twice.

The drive to the store was uneventful, despite Alice being paranoid about the black car following her.

Officer Rivera hadn't contacted her, and she doubted he would unless it directly concerned her. Who would be stupid enough to tell the police they'd been following a specific person? Although, based on some of the true crime shows she'd seen in the past, there were definitely criminals who were that stupid.

Pulling onto the street running behind the store, she swore she saw the black car parked on one of the side streets, but with the flow of traffic, she didn't have the opportunity to double check.

Locking the garage door, Alice went upstairs. Nothing looked out of place. At the front of the store, she peeked around the shade to see if Alistair or the black car were there. She didn't see either, so she took her purchases upstairs to set up the ward in the bathroom.

Sitting on the couch with the book Sage had given her, she skipped to the part about warding instead of reading it front to back like a novel. Learning all she could, she went into the bathroom and set up the stones. Placing each stone, she spoke her intent on why she needed them and what she wanted protection from.

The amethyst went closest to the shower and bathtub because she spent more time in the tub than at the mirror. Once she felt as confident as she was going to get, she went into the dining room.

"Kyle?"

"It better be important. We were about to watch a spaghetti western." Kyle wore a cowboy hat with a pair of chaps and looked ridiculous.

"How are you able to watch a movie? Ghosts can't touch anything."

"No, but we've seen it so many times we can act it out ourselves. I'm the sheriff." He puffed out his chest.

"Good to know. I need your help with something. It'll be fast, but I don't know if it'll hurt you." For the most part, Alice had always been a pacifist and didn't like for animals or people to get hurt. She didn't want to see Kyle be hurt by her ward, but she was still undecided about Alistair.

"You can't hurt me. Whatcha got?"

"I need you to follow me and try to get into the bathroom."

"That's it? Through the door, or wall, or what?" Kyle side-eyed her as they went into the bedroom.

"Yes." Alice shrugged.

As Kyle tried the doorway, it was like there was a translucent wall keeping him back. Thankfully, he'd put his hand up first or else he would have run into it with his nose.

Alice still wasn't sure he couldn't be hurt, but it was one reason she was reading the book from Sage.

"What did you do?"

"Will you see if you can get through the wall, floor, and ceiling, please?" Alice smiled at him.

He disappeared and reappeared next to her within seconds. "I can't get in at all. Are you going to tell me what you did?"

"I will, but don't be mad."

"Why would I be mad? Did you talk to that witch, Sage something?" He folded his arms across his chest like a toddler about to throw a tantrum.

"I did. While I was out, I realized I didn't want ghosts hanging out in my bathroom while I was taking a bath."

"Can't say I blame you, but why Sage?"

"Because hers was the first occult store I came to, and she seems like nice lady."

"She's nice until you cross her, and then she isn't."

"Oh … should I not tell you I asked her to be a consultant for anything witchy or occulty which may come into the store?"

"You did what?" Kyle paced the room.

"We can discuss it later. You have a western to act in, and while I asked her, it doesn't mean she will A. actually be needed and B. will come over."

"True, I still don't like it, but it's your business now. I respect the fact you're seeking consultants for things you don't know and trust me, there are *a lot* of things you don't know."

"Geez, thanks for the vote of confidence, Kyle."

"I have confidence. I just know what Florida, especially St. Augustine, is like. Sorry, gotta go. There's a barmaid who needs rescued." He winked before disappearing.

Even the spirits have more exciting lives than I do.

Alice returned to the coffee table where the book was laid open. She knew she had either enough time to go downstairs and get some work done, or she could have an early dinner and read more.

Not wanting to upset the western taking place somewhere in the building, she instead spent time on herself. She wanted to read more so she could understand the other inhabitants of the building better.

Other than the chapter about wards, there wasn't a specific chapter Alice was interested in, so she started at the beginning. Sage was a talented writer, engaging while also informative.

Nathan had been a professor, so she knew how dry educationally focused material could be to read.

She came to a section about how a spirit could be tied or anchored to an object. They're unable to cross over and can feel it if the object is not being protected by wards or charms. It could explain why there were so many spirits in the building, due to all the antiques they could be tethered to. Either that or they enjoyed hanging out with Kyle. Alice assumed it was a mix of the two.

She felt her eyes drifting closed, so she put the bookmark in and left the book on the table.

Alice locked the door leading from the upstairs to the main floor and shut off the lights. Gazing out over the street from the guest bedroom, Alice saw the black car and someone standing next to it. The figure was standing in the dark between streetlamps, but she thought it could have been Alistair. But he was a ghost and shouldn't be that opaque.

I need to decide if it's a spirit or a ghost. I feel dumb using them interchangeably. Unless there really are two different types.

Alice watched the black car pull off. The figure melted into the alley they'd been standing near, so she couldn't tell who it was for sure.

Everything she knew, or thought she knew, about the world was being turned upside down. First ghosts, then what? Werewolves and Death? Kyle had already said Death exists, and that was more than enough.

Alice felt a headache come on from trying to wrap her head about everything she'd learned in the last week, or really since moving to St. Augustine, so she left the dark guest room and went to her room.

Lying in bed, she made a list on the notepad next to her bed of what needed to be accomplished tomorrow. Alice really hoped Cynthia would at least consider the job. She didn't know if there was a way for her to run the business by herself with how busy it was. Just as she was falling asleep, she heard a thud and her name being yelled.

"Alice, wake up. Someone's trying to kick the door in," Alice thought she heard Kyle say, but she must have been dreaming.

"ALICE." This time, she was sure she'd heard it. She heard another thud as she was getting out of bed. Without turning on the lights, she grabbed her phone and a flashlight and opened the door to the stairs. Creeping down, she fumbled to open her phone.

"911, what's your emergency?"

"Hello, this is Alice Tidway. I own Forgotten Echoes at 10 Aviles Street. I believe someone's attempting to kick the side door in."

"Where are you right now, ma'am?" The sound of the dispatcher typing in the background carried through the phone.

"I'm walking down the stairs from the second floor."

"Do you have any weapons on you?"

"No, only my phone and a flashlight."

"Please go back upstairs. The police are en route."

Alice considered what the dispatcher had suggested but decided against their advice. Hitting the landing, she looked toward the side door. There was light radiating around the frame, as if someone was shining a flashlight toward the door. She felt drawn to the door and had taken a step forward when Kyle materialized next to her.

"Don't," Kyle insisted.

Before she could argue, she saw the red and blue lights flashing through the blinds. She heard a car come to a screeching halt before a door slammed. Yelling and shouting could be heard right before something hit the side door, hard. It felt like an hour, but ten minutes later, she heard a knock on the door. Alice opened the door to find Officer Rivera standing in the doorway, scowling.

"I thought dispatch told you to stay upstairs?" He growled as he crossed the threshold.

"And if I had, I wouldn't have heard you knocking," Alice countered.

"Good point. Is there any damage that you know of?"

"They didn't get inside, so there isn't on this side of the door, but I haven't checked the outside of the door yet. Do you know why someone would try to kick in my door?"

"Who did you piss off?" Rivera smirked.

"No one that I know of. I've just been selling antiques and keeping my head down." Alice glared.

"Another officer is interviewing him, but he says he was paid to break in and grab something."

"Any idea what that 'something' is?"

"No, but has anything else happened that I should know about?"

Alice explained the phone calls and the general unease after Trent had come into the store.

"Thank you. I'll make sure all this is added to the report, and hopefully, the calls were just teenagers pranking you." Officer Rivera shook Alice's hand before going to leave. He paused at the doorway and turned back to her. "One last thing. Are you the only one inside right now?"

"As far as I know, why?"

"The man we arrested was going on about a man he saw in the window."

"There's absolutely no man in any of my windows."

Officer Rivera tipped his head slightly. "Thank you. If anything else happens, please let us know immediately."

"Will do, thank you." Alice climbed the stairs, wondering why the man was talking about a man in the window but shrugged it off as something someone on drugs would say.

Falling into her bed, she fell asleep thinking about all the inventory she still needed to deal with. In the darkness of her room, she didn't notice the figure standing near the doorway to the living room. His eyes flared red for a split second before he turned and disappeared.

Chapter Nine

Alice knew she had a lot to do when she woke up, but she wasn't worried. Since it was only 10, she had a good seven hours of work time ahead of her if she wanted to be done before it got too late.

She carried her tea down to the main floor after she ate her brunch. She cracked her neck as she flipped the switch to turn the lights on. The store was dark without the sun shining in, so she opened the blinds but kept the door shade down. If the big 'closed' sign wasn't enough to stop people, she couldn't help them.

During her inventory of what was left in the front, she was surprised. Almost nothing she'd brought up from the basement was still there. Some of the larger pieces remained, as she'd expected. Most of the small and medium size antiques were new to her.

When she finished organizing, she drained her tea and turned her sights to the stockroom. Unfortunately, before she could get started, she heard a knock on the front door.

She glanced around the shade and saw Cynthia.

Alice unlocked and opened the door. "Hey, I didn't know if you'd come."

"I had a serious conversation with my husband, and he agreed I need something with less drama than the title office, especially if it pays more."

"I understand. Did you want to start today? We'll be closed on Mondays and Tuesdays, and if you don't want to work full time, you don't have to. You can work part time if that works better for you." Alice felt like she was word vomiting.

"No, I want to work full time. Have you set your hours yet?"

"Now that you're here and want to work, let's go over by the counter, and we can talk about it." Alice pulled a chair from the office, and they sat behind the counter.

"I'm not a morning person. If needed, I can be, but I like to get up at around ten and then go to work. What do you think about moving the hours to later?" Alice waited for Cynthia to respond.

"You want my input?"

"Yes, I may own the business, but if you're working for me, I want you to have as much of a say in how things are done as I do. Honestly, there will probably be pieces you know more about than I do. It'll give me more time to handle accounting and billing." Alice meant everything she'd said. She didn't want her employee to feel like they were *just* an employee.

"Wow, Ms. Smalls never asked for my opinion. Knowing St. Augustine the way I do, I think you have two primary groups. You have the morning walkers and shoppers who tend to be older, and you have the afternoon and evening tourists who are generally younger with families. I think business will be slower in the early morning, pick up at around 11, and be steady until five or six. We may have pockets of locals who come through after that."

"Are you a morning person? Night owl? What does your husband do for work? I want to make sure you have a good work-life balance. I know there were times when Nathan and I were younger when it seemed like he worked all the time. Do you have kids? Sorry, I know this is a lot of questions, and I don't want you to feel as though you have to answer all of them."

"It's fine. Might as well play 20 questions now versus over the course of the day, right? I'm a morning person and usually up by six or seven. My husband, Jake, works at the ports here and in Jacksonville, so his hours are all over the place. He usually works 70 hours a week, so we see each other when we can. He's considering getting a management position, so instead of doing all the hard work himself, he can tell everyone else to do it. If he does, he'll have two days a week we'll know for sure he doesn't have to work. But I won't believe it until I see it."

"How about we open at nine with you, and I come down at noon? You can work until five, and I'll close up at seven? To get your full hours, and possibly overtime, you can come in on the days we're closed to help get everything ready for the week, as well stay later if we're slammed," Alice thought out loud.

"Great. We're looking at buying a house soon, so having a higher hourly rate and the possibility of overtime will really help."

"My plan for today was to get the stockroom organized and inventoried. While I get started, do you want to speak with Francis? He's my accountant and does all the financials for the business. He'll get all the paperwork started and make sure you're paid." Alice and Cynthia stood.

"Thank you for this opportunity. I've always loved history."

"No, thank *you*. I need the help, especially after last weekend. I may not be old, but I'm too old to be running back and forth all day, every day."

Cynthia laughed at Alice's comment as Alice found Francis' number.

"Here. Use my phone. I'll give him a call, bring him up to speed, and you can talk to him after." Alice dialed Francis' office, knowing he would be there.

After explaining the situation to Francis, Alice handed the phone to Cynthia and smiled before she left to go to the stockroom.

In the stockroom, she put her hands on her hips and took in everything.

There were antiques spilling off the shelves and out of boxes. It looked like the *Antiques Roadshow* threw up all over the room.

"Kyle," Alice called quietly so Kyle could hear her, but Cynthia couldn't.

"Yes? Who's the girl up front?"

"Her name's Cynthia, and she's going to be working here, at least for the next six months, if the weekend was any indication of how business is going to go."

"It'll be this busy. Antiques hold a special place in people's memories and hearts." Kyle smiled at her, and Alice noticed the cowboy hat was gone, thankfully.

"Speaking of antiques, this place is a mess. What do you know about what, or who, brings the boxes here?"

"Things just appear. I think it's the building. It's been this way for as long as I can remember."

"I guess we need to have a conversation with the building because I'm not going to be okay with a constant mess back here. What if someone wants something specific? It's not like I could find it."

"No. The store knows what someone's looking for, finds the item, and puts it where it's needed for them to find it. I always saw a soft shimmer around an object which was ready to be placed with its new owner, but I'm not sure if you'll be able to. But I have a suggestion. If you put labels on the shelves, stuff will stay in its assigned area."

"What do you mean, Kyle?"

"If you have a shelf saying 'Christmas Angels', all the Christmas angels will appear on the shelf instead of scattered through the room. I had labels on some of the shelves, but it looks like they were removed after I died."

"I'm glad we're getting somewhere. You have labels in the office?"

"Of course. They're in the second drawer on the right. Assuming the realtor didn't move them," Kyle grumbled toward the office.

"I doubt it. At least, not from what I saw. Kyle?"

"Yes, Alice?"

"Tara asked me something, and it got me thinking. Did you ever pay anyone for any of this inventory? Meaning, did you ever receive invoices for any of it?"

"Nope. I know some of it was going to be thrown away. There were a couple of instances where the family of the original owner came in and was surprised to see it because they'd planned to throw it away, but it was gone when they'd tried to find it."

"Good to know. I don't want a random bill from some strange company asking for finder's fees showing up."

"The only one talking about a finder's fee is Death. Occasionally, he'll bring in something he wants you to hold on to, and he wants something in return."

"Like what? My soul?" Alice laughed and realized Kyle wasn't joining in.

"Death doesn't take souls. Not like in the movies, anyway. That's the reapers' job. He wants information on who the item goes to."

"Should I be keeping track of who buys what?" Alice hadn't considered keeping track of who purchased what, but if there was other necessary accounting, she needed to know now.

"No, only on certain items. There's a book somewhere in the office where all the sales are automatically recorded, along with the information about the buyer, so you don't have to."

"You mean to tell me there's a book recording everything on its own? Who fills it out? Why haven't I found it yet?" Alice wanted to dig through the office again but knew organizing the stockroom was more important.

"The store fills it out. It's part of its charm. Don't know where it is, but it should be somewhere in the office. I'll poke around while you work on this." Kyle motioned toward the stockroom. He disappeared right as Cynthia came into the room.

"I've finished up with Francis." Cynthia gingerly stepped around boxes to get to Alice. "Wow, this place is a mess."

"No kidding. This is my primary goal for today, but you know what I was thinking? We should label the shelves and organize from there. I think it may work better."

"Sure. I can start moving things away from the shelves if you want to make the labels." Cynthia was already pushing a box with her foot.

"There should be labels in the office. Which, have you seen it? It's a project for another day. The basement is too." Alice laughed as she left Cynthia moving boxes to one side of the room so they could start on the other side.

In the office, she found the labels in the drawer Kyle had said they should be in. Before leaving, she scanned the office. Her view fell on an old ledger with the word "Sales" written in large letters on the cover. Rolling her eyes at the store while she thanked it, she left to join Cynthia, waving the labels and sharpie triumphantly.

"Given what this room looks like, you finding those was faster than I expected. I figured everything was just as cluttered as it is in here." Cynthia had moved enough boxes for them to organize the stockroom.

"While you were moving the boxes, did you see anything you thought should be on a labeled shelf?"

"Clocks, stuffed animals, kitchen utensils, and books were the things I saw the most of at first glance."

"Perfect. We'll start there and make more labels as we clear things."

Alice made the first four labels and attached them to the shelf. For the next hour, she and Cynthia sorted through boxes, made smaller piles of other similar items, and found enough clocks and books to fill the entire store.

"I think we should take a break. We've been at this for a solid hour. Want something to drink?" Alice dusted off her hands.

"That would be fantastic, but how about we go down to Sweet Scoops and get something there instead?"

"I like it. Have you had ice cream from there before?"

The women gathered their things from the counter and stepped outside.

"Yeah. My uncle's ex-wife owned the building next-door to us; the one with 'Old Stone' sign. I haven't seen her in a long time, not since they divorced. I used to come down here all the time."

"Your family doesn't own it anymore?"

"I don't know, but it was a long time ago. I think I was maybe seven or eight, and my parents would bring me down here to see them. Sometimes we got ice cream if my brother and I were behaving."

"Younger or older brother?" Alice held the door open for Cynthia.

"Older, and he's a pain in the ass, but don't tell him."

"Wouldn't dream of it." Alice laughed as the cashier at Sweet Scoops welcomed them inside. "Are you wanting a drink, or would you rather have a small ice cream? My treat, of course."

"Thanks, but I couldn't. It wouldn't be fair if you bought my drink or snack on top of giving me a job."

"I insist.

Alice didn't want to hold up the line. After ordering two drinks and small cones, Alice and Cynthia waited for their refreshments at a nearby table.

"I have a small speaker I carry in my car. Do you want me to bring it in? It might help pass the time," Cynthia offered as they left the ice cream shop.

"That's a great idea."

"Please don't tell me you listen to Bach." Cynthia shuddered.

"Who do I look like? The Crypt Keeper?"

"Who?" Cynthia cocked her head before bursting out laughing. "I'm joking. I know who that is."

"Good. If you weren't, I'd have had to fire you. I listen to most thing genres. Classical, folk, and reggae are the only things I don't listen to, I think. I lean more toward metal and rock."

"Like Jefferson Airplane?" Cynthia hid her laugh behind her hand.

Alice mock glared at her. "Why, yes. Them and The Pretenders." She rolled her eyes and shook her head as their drinks and food were delivered.

"I'm kidding. I like rock, pop, punk, metal, and a little country, so I think our music tastes will mesh well."

Turning to head back to her store, Alice saw the black sedan turn onto the road.

"Get to the store, now." Alice pushed Cynthia forward.

"What's going on?" Cynthia asked as Alice tried to unlock the door, and the car slowed to a stop in front of the store.

Alice shook her head. "Not right now."

Not wanting to create more of a scene, she rushed Cynthia inside and locked the door.

A few seconds later, there was a heavy knock on the door.

Alice whisper shouted, "Don't!" as Cynthia grabbed the doorknob to open it.

"Why don't you want me to open the door?"

"The black car outside? It's been following me for the last couple days, and other business owners on the street have reported it to the police. It's suspicious."

The knocking turned into a banging while Alice dug in her purse for Officer Rivera's card with his number. Finding it, she called as the noise escalated. She was sure other tourists on the street had stopped to see what was going on.

"This is Officer Rivera. Who, may I ask, is calling?"

"This is Alice Tidway. The black car that's been following me is stopped in front of the store, and now someone's banging aggressively on my locked door."

"Can you see who's knocking?"

"Let me check." Alice peeked around the shade. Much to her surprise, no one was there. The knocking was still occurring, but there was no one standing on the other side of the door, nor was the black car still there.

"The car is gone, but someone is still banging on my door."

"They left? Was it the same license plate?"

"I didn't see the plates, but I'm sure it was."

"I'll add it to the report. Be careful and make sure all the doors are locked." He hung up after Alice assured him she would.

"No one's out there?"

"Nope. You heard the knock and saw the black car too, right?" Alice didn't want her new employee to think she was crazy.

"I did. I can't believe someone was knocking so loudly, but then stopped and disappeared? So strange." Cynthia went over to the front door. "I almost forgot the speaker. Let me go grab it."

"Please watch out for the car."

"Will do." Alice let Cynthia out and looked both ways to see if maybe the car had only moved to where she couldn't see it from the door.

It was nowhere to be seen.

At least Cynthia had seen and heard it too, so she knew she wasn't going completely crazy.

A new knock on the door caused Alice to jump. She peeked out and saw Cynthia holding a tiny speaker. Laughing at herself, she let Cynthia in, and they went back to work.

When they got to the stockroom, they realized some of the boxes were empty, flattened, and stacked against the wall. The labeled shelves were fuller than when they had taken a break. Alice glanced around the room.

Kyle was right. Apparently, things not only show up, but they put themselves away too. That's pretty convenient.

"I hadn't realized we'd gotten so much done. We have what? Five more spaces on the shelves on this side of the room and then nine on the other? We might be able to knock out this whole thing today." Cynthia plugged in her speaker and put it near the back wall.

"Maybe we need to take breaks more often." Alice joked. Wishful thinking and all that.

"The next two labels are…" Cynthia scanned the room as Alice stood, posed with labels and sharpie. "…tea pots and cups, and bells."

"Bells?" Alice wrote it down.

"Like those collectible decorative bells people display?" Cynthia held up a small white bell before shaking it gently. A soft tinkling came from it.

"I didn't know they were still a thing." Alice picked up another bell sitting on top of a box.

"My great-grandmother had some, but I didn't know people still collected them. The previous owner must have kept an inventory of them."

They continued sorting until Alice's phone rang from a number she didn't recognize.

"Hello?"

"Hi, is this Alice Tidway?"

"Yes, it is. Who is this?"

"Hi, I'm Trent Benson's attorney, Nancy Levitt. According to him, you have something of his, and he wishes for it back. I wanted to call you and try to resolve this before I got the police involved."

"I remember meeting him when I first arrived. I've just purchased the property, so you must understand I don't have a full inventory just yet. Do you know what he's misplaced? When Mr. Benson was here, he didn't or refused to tell me what he was looking for. Let's not glaze over the fact he broke into my store." Alice wasn't in the mood to go back and forth with an attorney. If she needed to, she could get Darcy involved, but considering she still didn't know what she was supposedly in possession of, Darcy would likely tell the attorney to take a flying leap.

"I apologize. I thought he'd told you. No, he didn't tell me what it was, only that it holds both significant monetary and sentimental value."

"Ms. Levitt, I'll be honest with you. I've spent the entire day getting one part of this building organized. So far, between me and my employee, we have moved probably over 200 items. If I don't know what I'm looking for, I can't tell you if I have it. As I told Mr. Benson, I'd be happy to return his item, but until someone tells me what I'm looking for, I cannot help you."

"I understand. I'll let my client know. If I find anything out, I'll be in contact."

"Thank you. Have a good day." Alice hung up. "I'm sure he's going to tell you exactly what it is." She rolled her eyes.

"Were you talking to me?" Cynthia came out of the stockroom.

"No. This guy came in before I was even open to demand I give him something he said was his. His attorney was calling to ask for the same thing."

"What's he looking for? I could be on the lookout."

"Funny you should ask. Neither the man, nor his attorney, seem to know what he's misplaced."

"Wait, what? He wants something but doesn't know what it is?"

"He either doesn't know or doesn't want anyone else to know what he's looking for. Either way, I can't help him unless he answers our questions. How's it looking back there?"

"Good. I'm taking a quick break, and I'll get back to work. It's almost time for more labels. By the way, what's the man's name?"

"Take your break, and we can talk about it when you get back."

Alice went into the stockroom by herself. "Kyle?"

"What? Wow, this place looks noice."

"Really? Noice? What are you? 16?"

"I learned it from a new ghost. I think it's fitting. Anyway, what do you need?"

"Can you think of anything Trent Benson may have left here, or you were given for him? His lawyer called."

"I'll think about it." Kyle left.

He usually stayed longer, but Alice thought maybe it was because of Cynthia. It's not like she could see him.

"Hey, so the guy's name?" Cynthia picked up a box on the way in.

"His name is Trent Benson."

"Is he's about five feet three inches, 300 pounds, and kind of a jerk?"

"How did you know?"

"He's well known around this area. He calls himself the 'high lord' of some church."

"Do you know what kind of car he drives?" Alice was already thinking Trent may be the person who's been following her. Especially now that he'd had his lawyer contact her, but she wanted to be sure.

"He doesn't, as far as I know. I know he has a driver, or at least did, but I doubt he knows how to drive. Probably thinks he's too good for such simple things."

"You know anything else about him?"

"Not really. I know he's creepy. When I was growing up, there were tons of whispers about his church. They tried to recruit kids from the middle school."

"How weird. Thanks." Alice checked the time. "What time did you want to get out of here tonight? We've made a really big dent in the mess and even more so with you working tomorrow."

"I was thinking another hour or so. We should be able to get this side all labeled and done and start on the other side later."

"Sounds good to me. I don't want to overwork you so soon after you start."

"I'm used to hard work. Or at least, I was when I was growing up. Even while working at the title business, it was more mental work, but for me, it was more tiring than this. Just think, after a month or two of lifting heavy boxes, I'll be in much better shape."

"I'm probably going to take a bath tonight to relax. I can feel my arms already aching."

The last three labels were radios, snow globes, and small statues.

Alice couldn't stop thinking about Trent and whatever he was looking for. There had been nothing so far Alice thought could warrant such a strong demand. There were some things worth money, but nothing to have a lawyer call about.

As they finished one last box, Alice cringed at the stack of boxes.

"I think we're good for today. Help me break down all these boxes."

"I don't think you should break them all down. People may need them if they buy a lot, or we may need boxes for more fragile items."

"Good point. Let's break some of them down. I worry if we keep them all, they'll refill themselves overnight."

Cynthia laughed at Alice's joke, but Alice was serious. Considering how much she didn't know about this building, she was truly worried when she came down in the morning every single box would have refilled.

"Don't forget your speaker," Alice reminded Cynthia as they came back in.

"We have several, so this one can stay here if you want."

"I probably won't be getting the store wide system for at least a month. Depending on how this week goes sales-wise, at least."

"Since we're half organized, sales should be even better than they were."

"Half? There's still an entire basement and office. Although, the office only has a safe with some things in it, so it's nowhere near as cluttered."

"I forgot about the basement. Will you show me tomorrow?" Cynthia checked her phone. "It's my lucky night. Jake's going to be home earlier than usual and said he'd cook dinner. He must've broken something at work. Either himself or some tool."

"I remember those days. Have a good night, and I'll see you tomorrow. Hold on, I have an extra key. I'll get it for you so you can open tomorrow morning. Unless you want me to work with you for the first day of sales."

"It's probably good if I take the key, but I think you being here for the first part of the day would be a good idea. Never having worked in retail, I don't want to mess anything up."

"I can be down here at eight forty-five to let you in. There isn't a lot of prep in the morning, and I can bring the coffee pot down. I'm more of a tea drinker."

"We could make room for it in the office. Or we can once the office is cleaned up."

Alice handed Cynthia the key.

"The key should work for the side door as well. I intend to get a keypad for the side door, eventually." Alice unlocked the front door and waited for Cynthia to step through the doorway.

"I'll see you bright and early. Or bright and early for you, anyway." Cynthia laughed as she headed to her car.

Closing and locking the door, Alice found Alistair standing in the middle of the store.

"Why hello, Alistair. How can I help you?" Alice didn't want to deal with a ghost, especially one who wanted something from her, and had lied to her. She had enough issues dealing with the living.

"Were you able to find my pocket watch? I need it."

"I found a few pocket watches, but I'm still organizing. Do you want to look through what I've found?" Alice wasn't lying. While she was sorting or selling things, if she'd come across a pocket watch, she held it back in the office in case it was Alistair's. Not like he could touch it, but maybe he wanted to see it.

"I guess." Alistair floated behind Alice as she pulled out the jewelry box full of pocket watches she'd stored in the office as a decoy to keep him away from the real one until she knew what was going on. Dumping them onto the counter, she moved them around so he could see each one.

"It's not here."

"Alistair, I think something is wrong with your memory."

"Why? Do you know something?"

"I found this." She pulled out the newspaper and showed him. "You said you were from Ohio, and you needed the pocket watch because your daughter had it with her when she died, so you thought it ended up here, right?"

"Yes, I think that's true."

"Then why are you on the front cover of this newspaper from Palm Coast about a parade you were in as the Grand Marshal? Do you remember?" She turned the paper so he could see it.

"What? No way. That's not me. I'm so confused."

"It *is* you. Your name is even in the caption. Is something else going on than you're telling me? *If* I find this pocket watch, what are you going to do with it? You can't hold or move anything."

"I was told I had to get the watch. It'll show the location of the box."

"Who told you that? What box?" Alice had a sinking feeling in her stomach the more he spoke.

"It's all so fuzzy. I don't think I'm supposed to know about the box. After being pulled from limbo, I was told I had to find this pocket watch."

"And you don't remember who told you to do it?" Alice didn't necessarily believe him, but if he said he didn't know, she had to at least listen.

"No, it's hazy. I'm not from Ohio?" He winced in pain.

"Are you alright?" Alice didn't know if she could even help him, or why he would be in pain.

"Every time I consider myself not from Ohio, it hurts. It hurts so bad." Alistair was almost doubled over in pain.

"You must be from Ohio, and this article is wrong." Alice tried to say something to help him.

"I'm from Ohio." The third time he said it, he stood straighter, the pain vanishing.

"Listen, I haven't gone through everything yet, but I don't think I have this watch you're asking about." Alice decided not to push the information in the newspaper article since it caused him pain to think about.

"Can you keep looking for it? I really need it."

"Do you remember if there's a photo inside the watch? Or any other information than what you told me the first time?"

"I think so, and the photo will be in color since my daughter didn't die very long ago. That's all I know, though."

"Thank you. I promise I'll keep my eye out for it," Alice said as Alistair dropped his head sadly before fading away.

"Kyle, I need you now."

"Alistair is gone. If you're calling me to find out."

"Thanks for coming to help. I think he's being controlled by someone or something." Alice scooped up the pocket watches and put them into the plain jewelry box used as a decoy for the one in the dumbwaiter.

"What makes you think he's being controlled?"

"When I told him about the newspaper article, anytime he tried to think about living in Florida, it was like he was being punched or stabbed in the stomach."

"You think his memories are being blocked and fake ones have been added?" Kyle scratched his chin.

"Is it possible? Seems like it to me."

"How odd. And you showed him the article? Did he say anything else about the watch?"

"I thought you were listening in?"

"With half an ear." Kyle shrugged when Alice glared at him.

"What's going on with you? You used to be here all the time and were damn near hovering, but today Cynthia and I were almost hit by the car, someone was pounding on the door, Alistair shows up, and you're here, but distracted."

"There are a lot of new people in and around the store, and I've been trying to be a good host."

"What do you mean, there are a lot of new people? Is it because of all the new stock?"

"No. Something else is going on. There are whisperings of things, but I haven't been able to get a clear answer."

"And you're only telling me this now? No thought about possibly letting the person who can see ghosts know something's going on that's causing more ghosts to show up?" Alice stormed toward the stairs.

"I'm sorry. This has never happened before. I think it's something to do with Trent and Alistair, though."

"Why do you think that?"

"Because it all started when you found the pocket watch and the other items."

"Shit. I almost forgot. Alistair said something about a box the watch was supposed to give the location of. What if they aren't supposed to be together?"

"I think it's a locating pocket watch. They are pretty common in the witching world."

"How do you know?"

"Before I kicked Sage out, I learned a few things from her."

Alice rolled her eyes. "Maybe I should call her." Alice went to the stockroom and opened the dumbwaiter. Shining her phone's light inside, she saw the jewelry box and the puzzle box. She closed the door and turned to see Kyle had joined her.

"Everything good?"

"Yeah, I don't have a good feeling about this."

"I don't either, but if ghosts are coming here, then it must be safe here, right?"

"Hopefully." Alice didn't know if she agreed with his assessment, but she couldn't worry about it at the moment.

"I don't think you should tell Alistair you have it."

"Oh yeah, I'm totally going to tell a ghost who we think is being controlled by someone that I have the thing they're probably all looking for. How dumb do you think I am?" Alice held up her hand. "Don't answer."

He laughed before disappearing, leaving Alice alone in the stockroom. With any luck, she'd find some answers in the book upstairs.

Taking the steps two at a time, she threw leftovers into the microwave and grabbed Sage's book. Skimming the table of contents, she didn't see anything screaming, 'bound ghost'. She was debating what to do when the microwave dinged. Noticing the time, she figured Sage should still be at her store, so she dialed the number.

"Whispering Wondyrs, this is Sage speaking. How may I help you this fine evening?"

"Hi, Sage. This is Alice from Forgotten Echoes, the antiques store downtown. I bought the stones from you?"

"Hi, please don't tell me the stones didn't work."

"They seem to work fine. I have another question. Have you ever heard of a ghost being bound to someone?" Alice didn't know how else to ask it.

"What do you mean? Hold on. Let me grab some books." Alice heard Sage put the phone down. "Alright, I'm back."

"Are we still talking theoretically, or did something happen?"

"Let's go with the second one." Alice wasn't completely sure she was ready to admit she saw ghosts, but Sage believed they existed.

"What's going on?"

"I have a ghost who's looking for something. He was extremely vague about the item. I later found evidence he'd been lying about some of the details he gave. The second time he came in looking for the same thing, he alluded someone brought him from limbo to have him find it."

"What was he looking for?"

"A pocket watch."

Alice heard a sharp gasp over the phone.

"Sage are you still there?" Alice asked when Sage hadn't said anything for a while.

"Yeah, um, did he say anything about it?"

"It was gold and oval with a symbol on the front."

"Was it triangles?"

"Maybe, why?"

"We need to talk, but not over the phone. I'm stuck here until my employee comes back on Friday. Are you available Saturday?"

"I am. I hired someone so I can take time off when I need to. If I find this watch, should I give it to him?"

"He shouldn't be able to touch it, and under no circumstances should you give it to him if you come into possession. Do you understand?"

"That's not cryptic at all, but I won't."

"Also, if you do see ghosts, not saying you do, but if Kyle the old owner is still around, you need to ask him if he has somewhere warded in the event you find the pocket watch. I don't mean like your bathroom, but higher power wards. He'll know, or at least he should. Not saying you've talked to him or anything. Crap, I have to go; a customer is here. Be careful." She hung up before Alice could say goodbye.

Alice didn't like what Sage had said and was wavering between believing her and being truly worried, and thinking the whole thing was fake. As she ate, she thought about the building and where a secret place could be. The safe? But the safe was too obvious of a place. Yes, after putting her plate into the sink, she decided it was easier to ask the man himself.

"Kyle, I need your help."

"I love hearing someone still needs my help." Kyle appeared near the couch. Seeing the book on the table, he walked over and looked at the cover.

"A published author, interesting. I wonder if it talks about how she can make mistakes." Kyle looked up.

"I haven't gotten far enough to know, but is there a room or shelf or place you've had warded?"

"You mean somewhere others can't see?"

"I guess."

"Who have you been talking to?"

"I called Sage and asked her some basic questions. Nothing about you or any other ghost, per se."

"Uh huh, if she comes stomping in here with her 'equipment', I will learn how to throw stuff at her real quick."

"Stop. Answer the question." Alice raised her voice. Her head hurt, and she wanted to shower and go to bed, but she needed answers tonight so she could be more prepared in the morning.

"I don't know. I'm sure somewhere here must be safe."

"Do you think it's the safe?" Alice wracked her brain about where it could be and whether she'd already found it.

"Maybe." Kyle held up his hands.

"Thanks, I'm going to bed." Alice watched Kyle disappear.

Grabbing the book, threw it onto the bed before taking her shower. She had to be up early in the morning to let Cynthia in, but hopefully she could sleep in a bit more after. A chapter and a cup of tea later, and she was asleep.

Nathan came to her in her dreams.

Love, you need to be careful. There are things you don't understand happening in town.

Tell me what's happening, so I can be prepared.

I don't even know everything, but from what I'm hearing, there's someone trying to unleash Gods onto the world.

What do you mean? Like they're trying to bring about revelations?

No, like Mount Olympus.

Why do I have to be the one to stop them? Aren't there people who are much more qualified than a middle age, perimenopausal woman who owns an antiques store?

Funny you should mention that. Apparently not. You're the one to do it. Along with help from your friends.

You quoting musical lyrics now? Alice felt the same bit of frustration she'd felt when Nathan would do this type of thing when he was alive. He would either not have all the answers or not give her all of them. It was like he wanted her to figure it out on her own, and she was tired.

No love, I'm serious. Lean on those you've met and those you'll meet to help you. You've always been strong and independent, but it's time to let others help you.

Fine, whatever.

Good girl. Get some sleep. Nathan faded before Alice could stop him.

She liked when he came to see her in her dreams. She knew it wasn't really him but her mind conjuring him, but she still liked it.

The rest of the night, she slept hard, not dreaming about anyone or anything.

Chapter Ten

The next morning went smoothly, and for the next three days, Alice worked alongside Cynthia during the day and read and studied at night. She thought maybe the whole Trent and Alistair thing was over because she hadn't seen the black car or either man. She knew owning a business wouldn't be easy, but with how busy it had been, she didn't have time for much else.

The weekdays weren't as busy as opening weekend, but she'd made enough to justify having an employee several times over.

Cynthia really seemed to enjoy the work.

Labeling the shelves had been the best idea they'd had. One side of the room was clear, and it finally allowed Cynthia and Alice to go in and out, grabbing stuff without risking life or limb. Thankfully, the side door had always been free of the ever-expanding mountain of antiques.

Alice's muscles were finally getting used to the amount of work she'd been doing. Stretching, she worried about Cynthia downstairs alone. She didn't know how busy it was and didn't want Cynthia stuck there all alone. She was glad because as soon as she stepped onto the sales floor, she saw the place was packed.

Jumping into action, she pulled items off the shelves and out of boxes to resupply while Cynthia handled the customers. They were so busy, they barely had time to nod to each other in passing. Alice was constantly going from the store to storage and back.

On one such trip, after stacking the new merchandise on a table, Alice went to go gather more when Cynthia stopped her with a vacant expression on her face.

"Are you okay?" Alice paused next to her.

"The police are here." She gestured to the front of the store.

Alice quickly shifted to see Officer Rivera in uniform and another man dressed in civilian clothing but with a badge at his waist. In between was Trent Benson, wearing a smug smile.

"You keep working with the customers. Don't worry about going to get more stock. After they leave, we can close for an hour if we need to." Reassuring Cynthia, she straightened and approached the officers.

"Good morning, officers. How can I assist you today?"

Officer Rivera wouldn't look Alice in the eyes, so she knew something was up.

"Is there somewhere we can speak more privately?" the other officer asked.

Alice stayed quiet but spun on her heel and led them to the stockroom. When she entered the stockroom, she noticed the place was still clean. Thanking the store for not showing its proverbial ass, she put her hands on her hips.

"What can I do for you today?"

"Mr. Benson says you have an item of his, and he would like it returned."

"And you are?"

"I'm Detective Levitt." He pulled out a pen and notepad and took notes.

"Are you related to Mr. Benson's attorney by chance?" Alice saw him stumble while writing for a second before he continued.

"I'm not sure. Levitt is a common name in this area."

Trent looked between Detective Levitt and Alice before whispering to Detective Levitt, "What do you mean you don't know? Why am I paying your godawful attorney of a wife if—"

"That's enough Mr. Benson." Detective Levitt turned and glared at him.

Alice pretended not to hear what Trent was saying, so she carried on the original conversation, "Oh, I wouldn't know; I'm new here. Yes, Mr. Benson came to my store before I was open to inquire, rather aggressively and despite of a locked door, on his belief I had something of his. If you didn't know, I recently purchased this property and moved here from Oregon. I didn't know Mr. Benson prior to him coming into my store uninvited, nor did I know if the store held something of his. When I asked him what he was seeking, he refused to tell me." Taking a deep breath, she continued.

"Every bit of the inventory you see came with the store. I sorted through most of it over the last week or so, at least on this floor. Recently, Mr. Benson's attorney called, claiming the same thing. Supposedly, I have something belonging to her client. I told her the same thing I'm about to tell you. If Mr. Benson tells you, his lawyer, or me what he's looking for, I will see if I have it in my possession. Here's the thing though, since he can't, or won't, tell me what it is, nor could his attorney, and I've been open for five days now, there's a good chance it's been sold."

"How dare you! You don't know who you're dealing with." Trent lunged at Alice, who stepped backwards.

"I appreciate your honesty. With your permission, may I look around?" The detective inspected the shelves.

"Do you know what Mr. Benson has misplaced?" Alice leaned against the wall.

"I didn't misplace it, you cow. It was removed."

Alice arched an eyebrow but didn't respond to his taunt.

"Detective, if we don't know what we're looking for, why would we look for it? How do we even know what to look for?" Rivera spoke up for the first time.

"You're right. Give me a minute." Levitt pulled out his phone and left the group. He made a call, finished, and returned within minutes. "We have a warrant incoming. You don't have to close, and the police will all be in plain clothes, except for Rivera here."

"You have a warrant for something this man" — Alice motioned toward Trent — "says I have, but won't tell you what it is? That's interesting."

"I was told by my superiors they have a warrant, so I'm not sure." Detective Levitt's eyes shifted between the people standing.

"I hope you understand, but I'll need my lawyer to review the warrant. You can either browse in the front as a customer or leave the premises until they've finished." Alice felt braver than she had ever before.

"We'll wait in the front and browse." Levitt practically had to pull Trent away from the stockroom.

"What? You aren't going to look now? What am I pay—" Trent started, but Levitt grabbed his arm and stopped his sentence.

Alice knew he was about to say 'paying', and it pissed her off.

"Mr. Benson, we must follow the law. Please don't make a scene. Ms. Tidway, you'll need to stay in the front with us to ensure you don't somehow remove the belongings of Mr. Benson." They left the room, with Rivera following.

"How am I supposed to not remove belongings allegedly owned by Mr. Benson if I don't know what the hell the belongings are to start with?" Alice called after them.

No one bothered to respond as she stormed past Cynthia, who was helping a customer at the counter.

"I need to make a phone call. I'll be in the office with the door open if they show up with their warrant before I come out."

Cynthia acknowledged, and Alice called Darcy to let her know what was about to happen.

"Alice, long time no talk. How are things in sunny Florida?"

"They were good up until I was informed I have a bunch of police on their way with a search warrant."

"For what? You just got there. Did the realtor not reveal something?"

"The realtor didn't reveal much. Like a whole other floor or the fact the inventory fills a space from floor to ceiling. No. It's this man who thinks I have something of his, but he won't tell me what it is, so he's having his lawyer, and now a police detective, try to get me to admit to having something when I don't know what it is."

"Weird, the search warrant should say exactly what they're looking for. When they get there with it, send me a photo of the warrant, but don't let them look at or touch anything until after I've confirmed it's legit."

"They're wandering around the front of the store in the same area as the customers for right now. Should I have made them leave?" Alice worried she had done something wrong.

"No, if it's in public view, they can look all they want. It sounds like you've had run-ins with this man before. Do you have time to give me the entire story?"

Alice gave Darcy a quick synopsis of what had happened over the last week. "He said the others will be here soon with the warrant, so I want to be off the phone by then. Thanks for everything."

"I'm your lawyer; you don't have to thank me. I'll speak to you soon, but I want to do some research before you send me the warrant."

Alice ended the call and went back to the counter. "I'm going to need to be at the counter, but if you want to grab more stuff, you can."

Levitt had told her she couldn't move anything or mention Cynthia not being able to. He'd also said they could leave the business open, and restocking was part of running the business.

Cynthia finished what she was doing and went to the back.

Alice heard Trent screeching about how 'her employee is going to destroy evidence!'

She rolled her eyes and placed a hand on Cynthia's shoulder.

"Hang on a minute. I'm going to make some things clear to the detective."

Alice approached Levitt as he attempted to get Trent under control.

"Detective Levitt, I feel I was being amicable by allowing you to stay in the building until the warrant came through, but as you can see, this is a small store. Most of our inventory is in the back. You told me I couldn't leave the front, therefore, my employee needs to in order to keep our stock on the sales floor. Mr. Benson is causing a scene, and I'm going to have to ask you to leave if you can't get him under control." Alice didn't wait for a reply before spinning sharply and stalking back to the counter. This was the first time Alice had ever talked back to a police officer, and it made her feel powerful.

Cynthia was still standing near the counter when Alice returned.

"Go get more stuff. It's fine."

"Yes ma'am. I'll be back shortly." Cynthia practically jogged toward the back.

Alice stayed at the counter to continue helping customers, so Officer Rivera approached her. "I'm sorry about this. They told me we were coming in and questioning you about this so-called 'stolen' item. It's become a much bigger issue than I thought it would be. I'm sorry for not calling and giving you a head's up after how much harassment you've been receiving."

"As a gesture of good faith, and hopefully encouragement to leave, when Cynthia returns, you're welcome to check everything she brings out. I have no reason to lie, or to take something from a man I didn't know even existed until he barged through my locked door, accusing me of having something of his before my store was open or inventoried."

"I appreciate that. Thanks for being so understanding. I hope this is the last problem we have with him."

Cynthia returned carrying a box filled with various items.

"Please let Officer Rivera see what you've brought."

He poked around in the box, lifting several pieces and inspecting them.

"I doubt any of this is the item he's looking for. You can put it out, and he can see it as you do." Officer Rivera finished inspecting the contents of the box.

Smiling, Cynthia lifted the box and placed merchandise around the room for the customers.

"Since you're standing here while I'm making sure nothing disappears, did you find out who the black car belongs to?"

He flipped through his notepad and stopped about halfway through. "I did, but it was strange."

"Strange in what way?"

"The car is registered to a Mister Alistair Sinclair. He went missing about four months ago. Initially, his family thought he was just taking a break from everything and everyone, which he's been known to do from time to time. With him being gone for so long, and that his car hasn't shown up anywhere, he's most likely dead. We haven't found his body, but unless he's hiding from his family, he couldn't be the one driving it."

Oh, he's dead, alright.

Alice relaxed her face to keep from letting on she knew the name. "Was there any record of him selling it or having a family member who could be driving it?"

"No, I haven't found anything else out. I've spoken to his family, and none of them have seen the vehicle let alone driven it. They've said it went missing the same time he did. Have you seen it since the night you called me when someone was banging on your door?"

"I haven't. Whoever was driving it must have stopped, or like a certain Levitt named attorney and detective."

"Alice, we don't know that. I'll keep the police report open. If you see it again, call me or the station immediately. You still have my card with my number, right?"

Alice nodded and stared past Rivera. Five people entered the small store at the same time. The woman leading the group stopped and spoke to Levitt before coming to the counter.

"Ms. Tidway?"

"Yes?"

"I'm Detective Moss." She offered her hand to Alice.

Alice firmly gripped the offered hand. "Do you have the warrant? My lawyer requested I scan it and send it to her to verify. We can proceed when she's finished."

"She has ten minutes." Detective Moss handed her the folded piece of paper and joined Levitt.

Alice opened the warrant and quickly scanned it with the feature on her cellphone. Not seeing they were looking for anything specific, she sent it to Darcy.

"Does the warrant say what they're looking for?" Cynthia glanced at the warrant.

"Not that I saw when I skimmed it." Right after she responded, her phone rang.

"Darcy."

"Hey, Alice. I went through it, and it's a legitimate warrant, but it looks like they're looking for 'religious memorabilia', whatever that means. Usually, warrants are much more specific. Do you have any clue what it could be?”

“No, I haven’t even seen a cross, let alone anything I would consider religious.” Alice’s mind jumped to the items in the dumbwaiter.

Those must be what he’s looking for. They don’t appear to be religious, though.

“Even if you have the item, when you bought the store, everything became yours. We could fight it due to how vague it is, but since it doesn’t seem to be anything too valuable, I don’t think it would be worth the fight. It says they can search both the main floor and your residence.”

Alice wondered why it didn’t include the basement, but she didn’t mention it with Officer Rivera standing right there. She had no reason to not trust him, but she also didn’t know him well enough to trust him with something like this.

“I guess I’ll let them know they can get started now that you’ve okayed it. Also, I’m going to text you a question. Give me a minute or two.”

“I’ll keep my phone next to me. I have a meeting in 30 minutes, so if I don’t know the answer, I’ll respond after my meeting.”

“Thank you, Darcy.” Alice hung up and quickly tapped out the question before heading over to the woman and Levitt.

“After consulting with my attorney, she has instructed me to fully comply, so please let me know what I need to do.”

“Thank you, Ms. Tidway. If you could please show two of our technicians to the stockroom and two to your residence, it would quicken the process. Detective Levitt, Officer Rivera, and I will stay here in the main area. How long until you close?"

"I can close the store whenever it dies down a bit more. I don't have set hours yet, so if you need me to close, I can."

"It should be fine for right now, but I'd like someone to be at the counter with you or your employee to ensure the items being sold aren't what we're looking for. Do you have a safe?"

"I do. Would you like me to take you to it now or show the others where to go first?"

"Show the others, and you can open the safe for me after."

Four technicians with small bags followed Alice toward the back. On their way past the counter, Alice paused to speak to Cynthia.

"Cynthia, I need to show these people to the stockroom and upstairs. If you wouldn't mind staying at least until I get back, I'd really appreciate it. I know you needed to leave early."

"Alice, I'm not missing this. For once, I'll have something exciting to tell my husband." Cynthia laughed as she patted Alice on the shoulder and went back to the document she was creating on her laptop.

"What are you making?"

"I figured we should have a mailing list so people who visit can be emailed when we get new stuff. What do you think?"

"Fantastic idea. Keep up the good work." Alice motioned for the four to follow as she led them to the back.

"Here's the stockroom. As you can see, we're currently working on organizing it. Enjoy." Alice felt a little thrill seeing their reactions when the last two learned their task. Their eyes bugged out, and Alice figured they regretted their decision to go to work today.

"As for you two, please come with me." She opened the door to the stairs, worried for a minute the basement stairs would be there too, but they weren't.

Whew. Crisis averted.

Alice opened the door to her upstairs apartment and held it open for them to enter. "There are two bedrooms and two bathrooms, one on each side of the place with the kitchen, dining room, and living room in the middle. Do you have any questions?"

"I don't believe so, ma'am," the taller of the two said.

"There are calming stones in my bathroom. Can you please be sure not to move them? Their placement is important to me, and I'd really appreciate it."

"There shouldn't be a reason we'd need to. If we end up needing to move them, we'll let you know first."

"Thanks. I'll be downstairs." Alice was halfway down the stairs when her phone beeped, alerting her to a new text.

*It doesn't include the basement. Which means they're
not allowed to go down there.*

Exactly what Alice had thought. She left the door at the bottom of the stairs open, so when the techs finished upstairs, they couldn't go downstairs without someone knowing. She didn't think the two upstairs wanted to be there anymore than the two in the backroom, but at least their task was easier.

Back at the counter, the woman approached Alice. "You ready to open the safe?"

"Sure. It's in the office. I have no clue what's inside because I haven't had time to go through it yet."

The lady pulled on a pair of gloves as Alice unlocked the safe. Opening the heavy door, they peered inside, where they found approximately 10 small boxes. She pulled out each and placed them on the desk. Seeing another jewelry box sitting on a shelf inside, the woman motioned toward it.

"What's in there?"

"I told you. I have no clue what's in here, but I can ask Cynthia if she knows anything. We did have a customer fond of giving pocket watches to his wife come looking for one. I told him I'd put aside any I found or bought and give him first dibs. Cynthia may have put things aside."

"You have such a loyal customer after only being open a week?"

"I wouldn't call him loyal, but adamant about finding certain things. Much like Mr. Benson, only with manners. I'm not going to complain because he spends money every time he comes in." The lie easily rolled off Alice's tongue.

"I should look at those first, just in case."

Alice knew she would find nothing of interest, so she stood quietly as the lady gently dumped out the box and sorted through them.

"You know, he never told me what he was looking for, and didn't tell Detective Levitt or his lawyer, either. The warrant says 'religious memorabilia'. It's hard to help with such vague wording."

"I understand. My orders are to pull anything resembling religious in nature, and let Mr. Benson look at it."

"He must have a crazy amount of power in this town if he can get the police to do his bidding without even knowing what they're looking for."

She glared at Alice for a few seconds but went back to sorting through the watches. Not seeing anything she deemed important, she put everything back into the jewelry box and rifled through the boxes from the safe. Rings, bracelets, a watch, and two more necklaces.

"I don't see anything here. You can put this back into the safe while I go through the drawers." She opened the desk drawers while Alice packed everything back up and replaced it in the safe.

"Can I close the safe now?"

"Yes, and I haven't found anything in the drawers, so I think I'm finished in here. Do you have any other rooms on this floor?"

"There's a bathroom next door and a broom closet near the side door."

"Show me those so we can get out of your hair."

"I appreciate it." Alice opened the door to the bathroom.

The woman examined it briefly and backed out.

Alice also opened the broom closet for her. It was exactly how it had been when Alice opened it the first time after buying the property.

"It's clean. Do you want to come with me to the stockroom to see if they've found anything?"

"Sure. Cynthia is handling the front, so it's not a problem."

The techs were still sorting through the boxes with a small pile of random trinkets and items which could be considered almost vaguely religious. Alice admired a bronze paperweight of the Archangel Michael holding a sword that could be a letter opener in the pile. She wasn't overly religious, but a nice paperweight that doubled as a letter opener may find its place on her desk.

"Ma'am, this is all we've found so far. We have two more boxes to go through, but if you want to check it, you can. Do you have a box we can put it all in?" One tech motioned to the pile when she saw Alice and Detective Moss enter the room.

"No thanks, we'll make Mr. Benson do it since he's the only one who seems to know what we're doing all this for, and he refuses to share the information with anyone."

Alice's eyes widened at the woman. She'd thought the woman was just another lackey, but something in her tone told Alice she was tired of this game as well. "I have a box. Let me get one for you." Alice walked over and retrieved one large enough to fit the pile on the floor.

"We're done here. Let's pack it up and take it up front. Set it on the counter for him to deal with."

"Please don't put it on the counter." Alice stopped the two techs.

"Where would you like us to put it?"

"There's a table next to the counter. I don't want to disturb customers who are trying to make their purchases."

"They can set it on the table," the woman told the techs as they carried the items to the front. When they reached the door leading upstairs, the other two techs came down.

"Ma'am, there's nothing up there resembling anything religious."

"Thank you. You can join us up front." The woman followed the four techs to the front.

Alice wanted to ask if they'd touched the stones, but she could check after they left.

Trent was already at the table, digging through what they'd found when Alice reached the table. Cynthia was helping customers, but Alice could tell she was trying to listen to what was being said.

She's definitely a keeper.

Alice went up and stood next to Officer Rivera.

Turning to her, he raised an eyebrow.

Shrugging, she stood there waiting for Trent to get through the items.

"It's not here. She must have hidden it. Where is it, you cu—?" Trent turned on Alice.

Detective Moss interrupted him before he could complete his insult. "Mr. Benson, we have searched this store thoroughly, as well as upstairs. There's nowhere she could have hidden anything. If you gave us an example of what you're seeking, Ms. Tidway could be on the lookout for it." It was obvious she was exasperated from dealing with him.

"No, I know what it is, and it isn't here." Trent pushed all the merchandise off the table.

"Now that you've conducted your search and didn't find what you're looking for, I must insist you to leave before any more of my stock is damaged." Alice stiffened at Trent's actions.

"I'm sorry. Yes, we'll leave immediately." Moss waved to the four techs, and they left the store together.

Levitt and Trent were having a heated discussion near the table. Finally, Levitt grabbed Trent's arm and dragged him to the front door.

As Levitt and Trent approached the door, Sage came through it carrying a bag and whistling.

When Trent saw Sage, his eyes narrowed, and his mouth moved, but Alice couldn't make out what he said.

Sage ignored him and came to the counter.

"I saw all the police. Is everything good?" Sage placed a bag from Burger Buckets on the counter.

"Ms. Tidway, here, is a master criminal. She stole something before she even lived here. That takes talent!" Cynthia grinned.

"Cynthia!" Alice wasn't actually upset, but pretended to clutch her chest

"It's fine, Alice. Sage is my aunt's husband's cousin. I think?" Sage nodded as Cynthia justified her comment.

Alice brushed off the comment about them being related. "Cynthia, I'm sorry for keeping you longer than we'd discussed. If you want to go home, I can close the store on my own."

"It's fine. I have nothing else going on. I need to learn how to close if you're ever out of town, anyway."

"Good thinking. Sage, if you want to look around, I'll show Cynthia what I need done for closing, and then we can meet in the back."

"Don't mind me, I could get lost here. Take your time." Sage was already wandering around the store while Alice showed Cynthia what to do.

"You feel confident to close without me?" Alice felt like she was putting a lot of pressure on Cynthia, especially with the police coming by.

"Absolutely, I'll close up, and tomorrow I'll open like normal."

"The police coming and doing a search didn't scare you off?"

"Absolutely not. This is way more fun than working at the title business."

"I'm glad. You've been fantastic this week. One more day until a much needed two days off."

"You go hang out with Sage before she absconds with your store."

"Should I be worried about her stealing?"

"Oh no, she would never. She's just a pro at bartering."

"So am I, so we shall see." Alice laughed as Sage came back empty-handed.

Sage grabbed the bag of food and followed Alice to the back.

Thankfully, Alice had moved chairs to the side of the room earlier, so she pulled them out.

"So, police?"

"First, what did Trent say to you?"

"He said, 'you won't get your hands on it.'"

"What a weirdo. I wonder what he meant." Alice wondered how Trent and Sage could have met. They were from completely different worlds.

"If it's what I think it is, he'll never get it." Sage turned serious. "Did they find anything during their search?"

"Nothing he seemed interested in. So, what's going on, and why am I in the middle of it?"

"I don't completely know. He's usually pretty aggressive, but not quite like this. I assume whatever he's looking for, he needs by Vestal Virgin's ritual, which starts May 14 at midnight."

"What is this, 'Vestal Virgin's ritual', and why is it important?"

"It's also called the Ides of May and usually thought of as a day of warning. However, the Vestal Virgins would throw water in the Tiber River to ensure water and fertility. It holds religious significance for some faiths. He belongs to a fringe sect of the Thelema religion. Did you notice his ring?"

"It's a triangle but not at the same time."

"The symbol for the primary faith is two connected triangles. It's a pagan faith surprisingly popular around here."

"Wow. I've never heard of it before. What else do you know about them?"

"Trent believes there's a pocket watch that, when combined with his ring, can find a special box."

"A box? Random, isn't it?"

"Yes, and no. Supposedly, the box releases all the gods onto earth when opened."

"What type of gods are we talking? Like gods of wine and flowers, or gods of malice and war? Also, why would such a box exist?"

"The bad type, usually famine, pestilence, death, war, etc. Pestilence is also known as conquest, but they supposedly don't like being called conquest."

"Oh, like the four horsemen? Fantastic."

"As to why they have the box, from the research I've done, it was to protect mortals from immortals."

"So, is the box like a prison for the gods?"

"In a sense."

"What does the box look like?"

"No one truly knows. It should have the symbols of Thelema on it and should not be capable of being opened."

"Whoa. No, I don't have anything like that here. Why does Trent think you want it?"

"No clue, and I have no interest in such a box, if it even exists. I doubt it does. I think it's a story elders told their kids to keep them in line."

"Probably. Well, thank you for dinner."

"Of course. But listen, if you find a pocket watch with the Thelema symbol on it" — she raised her hand — "Which I'm not saying you have one. But if you were to have it, and you had a secret place in the building that was warded, keep it there. Don't open it for anyone."

"Anyone?"

"Anyone. Unless it feels right, and you'll know when you feel it."

"Gotcha, even though I doubt I'll ever come into possession of such an item."

"Ghosts and this building have a funny way of making things appear when you least expect it." Sage smiled as she picked up the trash to take with her.

"I can take the trash. Don't worry about it." Alice reached out to take it and noticed the Thelema symbol tattooed on Sage's wrist.

"Yes, that is a Thelema symbol." Sage saw Alice trying to sneak a peek at it.

"Why not tell me you knew more about Thelema, or is it Thelemism?" Alice watched Sage to see if she was going to deflect or tell the truth.

"Just Thelema, but honestly, either works. Because I didn't want you to think I have ulterior motives, because I don't. Trent, Alistair, and I used to be close. We were the founding members of Thelemism in this area. Things went sideways. It's a long story that I'll tell you later. Just know that I'm nothing like Trent and neither is Alistar."

"I appreciate you telling me, and I'm sorry if I was accusatory."

"I didn't take it that way, but thank you. If you need anything, let me know. Be safe, Alice. Apparently, the world is counting on you."

"No pressure, right?" Alice laughed while Sage smiled.

"Why are you still here? You were supposed to be closing up." Alice realized Cynthia was still straightening the store when they came out of the stockroom.

"I was going to, but four people came in, and I lost track of time."

"Go. I'll see you in the morning."

"Awesome. Thank you for hiring me. This really is the best job I've ever had."

"I'm glad you like it, Cynthia. Goodnight, Sage. Drive safe."

Alice watched as Cynthia and Sage left through the front door and heard the key lock the deadbolt. She shook her head and went upstairs.

"You handled the cops and Trent well." Kyle's voice jolted Alice out of her thoughts as she reached the second floor.

"Thank you, I guess. Where have you been all day?"

"Hanging out in the basement with everyone else and avoiding the cops. You never know when someone may have the sight and cause an issue."

"As far as I know, I think it's just me, but I found out what Trent is looking for and whose car has been following me."

"Do tell."

"The car's owned by our ghost, Alistair Sinclair. Obviously, he's not driving it. Whomever is, took it after Alistair's death approximately four months ago. Trent's looking for religious memorabilia, but Sage thinks he's really looking for the pieces in the dumbwaiter. Speaking of which, Sage is part of the same religion with the symbol Trent's looking for."

"Sage is a Thelemite?" Kyle seemed surprised.

"She has the tattoo, so maybe she used to be, but isn't now? Trent has the ring with only one triangle, which is from a fringe sect who wants to unleash gods onto earth."

"Deep. You've already been picked to save the world."

"I wouldn't go so far as to say I'm supposed to save the world. This whole thing could be a fight over something with nothing to do with actual gods."

"Perhaps, or it could be a lot more than what Sage is telling you. I don't trust her."

"I don't know anymore. Oh, did you know she's related by marriage to my employee, Cynthia?"

"No, but it makes sense. It seems like almost everyone around here is related to everyone, somehow."

"True. Well, I'm exhausted, and tomorrow's another day." She was already heading toward the shower when Kyle faded into the floor.

***

Alice heard faint music coming from downstairs. The music was louder near the stairs, so she assumed Cynthia had turned on the music. Changing into work clothes, she poured a cup of tea before going downstairs.

She'd been right; the music was coming from the stockroom while Cynthia was working the front and counter. There were only a few customers, so Alice didn't feel bad distracting her.

"Good morning. Anything else happen last night after I left?" Cynthia skipped to Alice when she saw her.

"No, it was mundane. Exactly the way I like it."

"Good. So far, everything's been calm here. Nothing to write home about. I have the music playing because it was dead earlier, and I needed something to break the silence." Cynthia laughed as she straightened a lamp shade.

"I think the music is a nice touch. I think I'll be in the office trying to make sense of what's going on in there until it gets busy."

"Sounds good. I think I'm really getting the hang of everything." Cynthia beamed.

158

"You are. Please keep this energy because I see an entire group of people who seem interested in coming inside." Alice pointed at a large group of elderly women who had stopped right outside the window.

"I'll call you if I need you." Cynthia rambled off to help a customer trying to get a painting off the hook it was hanging from.

Alice was tempted to open the dumbwaiter to make sure the items were still in there, but she was afraid Alistair or Trent would appear out of thin air as soon as it was opened. The dumbwaiter must be the warded location. Alice realized Kyle hadn't responded when she'd asked him before.

Feeling bad Cynthia was working alone, Alice helped as much as she could without getting in Cynthia's way. On a trip to the stockroom to get more pieces, Alice noticed it wasn't restocking as quickly as it originally had. It could be because it was now stored on shelves, so it wasn't as spread out across the room. Regardless of the reason, it didn't seem like it was coming in as quickly. "Kyle?"

"Yes?" Kyle materialized in the middle of the room.

"Is there a reason it doesn't seem as full back here as it has been?"

"There is. Have you seen the basement? It's a hot mess."

"Hot mess?"

"Same kid who taught me the word 'noice'. Anyway, the store ebbs and flows. I forgot to tell you, didn't I?"

"What do you mean?"

"Sometimes it's packed, and you can barely walk through the store. Other times, you need to go to estate sales and buy stuff. The store uses energy, so by going to estate sales, you recharge the energy."

"But why estate sales and not garage or other sales?" Alice wasn't making the connection.

"It has to do with emotions. Garage sales may work, but I didn't like them. They're usually just clothes and random crap no one wanted. Estate sales have much better options, and there are emotions, either from the individual who passed, or their family. At least that's what I assume. I didn't really think about it much since I enjoyed going to the sales, but now I do. I think it's related to how long."

"How long what?"

"How long it's been since you last went to an estate sale. Come to think of it, it always filled itself up more after I went to a sale. The longer I didn't go, the less stuff came in."

"Thanks for letting me know."

"Anytime. Anyway, how's everything going? It's getting crowded downstairs."

"What am I supposed to do with them?"

"I don't know. While I like guests, you know what they say about guests who overstay their welcome?"

"They start to smell."

"Exactly. Let's figure out what's going on and get them out of my way." Kyle slid down through the floor, making a goofy face on his way down.

Good thing I hired someone if I'm going to need to go to estate sales.

Alice carried out an armful of goods. She placed it on the counter for Cynthia, who was talking to a customer.

The rest of the day was spent with Alice bringing inventory to the store front when Cynthia asked for it, but it slowed the later it got.

At five, Cynthia popped her head into the office.

"Are you at a good stopping point? It's quiet out here, so I was thinking about heading home."

Alice stood and stretched. "Go home. I can close up and get everything done. You plan to be here tomorrow?"

"Of course. I was hoping we could finish the other side of the stockroom and hit the basement when we're done."

"Have you been down there yet?"

"I went down earlier, and I found something interesting. Let me find it."

Alice thought it was a little strange but followed her.

Cynthia pulled a frame from under the counter and handed it to Alice. "A customer was looking for a picture frame. We didn't have any in the back, so I went downstairs. Don't worry, they were the only ones in the store, and I had the register locked."

"I wasn't worried about it, but why did you save this for me?"

"Turn it over and you'll see."

Alice turned it over and saw the image of a much younger Trent, Sage, and Alistair standing in front of a building with the Thelema symbol on it. It wasn't black and white, but Alice could tell it was older, probably late 1970s, or early 1980s, by the grainy photo.

"Have you seen this building?" Alice rotated it so Cynthia could see the building in the photo.

"I can't remember, but I see Sage is familiar with the building. She wasn't close to the family. I only really know her from Christmas and family reunions."

"Did either of these men go to your family's events?"

"Absolutely not. Trent wouldn't have been invited, and I don't know who the other guy is. He looks familiar, but I'm not sure why."

"Why wouldn't Trent have been invited?"

"He thinks he's too good for everyone. The one time I remember seeing him, he looked down his nose at the rest of us. Sage talked about Alistair, but not much about Trent. When she did, it was also with a tone of distrust, if you know what I mean."

"I know that tone well. Thank you for letting me know. This is definitely interesting information. Go home, get some rest, and I'll see you tomorrow."

"Have a good night." Cynthia grabbed her purse and left, the bell jingling as the door closed behind her.

Seeing the photo reminded Alice of something, and since there were no customers, she called Sage.

"Hey, did I forget something?" Sage asked as she picked up.

"No, but I forgot to ask you about something yesterday." The feeling in Alice's stomach was conflicting. She felt she could trust Sage, but the photo and tattoo proved Sage knew more than she was letting on.

"Hit me."

"Two-part question, actually. How do I know if someone is bound to an object, and if they are, how do I separate them?"

"Do you mean like an object came in, and there's a ghost attached to it?"

"Mostly."

"You can tell because when you touch the object, it brings the ghost forward. Another way is if the object is warded, and when you bring it out of the protected location, the ghost appears not long after."

"If the ghost appears, I'll know they're bound to the object? Does this happen if anyone touches it or just certain people?"

"It doesn't happen to everyone. Only to people who can communicate with ghosts. But you can learn to tune them out. Usually, a ghost will appear if there's one bound to an object. There are a few other reasons, but being bound is the most common."

"How do I break the binding?"

"Easy. There are five ways, but the easiest is to have a container full of salt, and you cover the object entirely with the salt."

"Sounds easy if the item is small. What are the other ways?"

"You can cleanse it with sage. If you know where it originally came from, you can return it. You could also bury it in a graveyard or burn it. The graveyard is the trickiest because it must be an old graveyard, not a cemetery, and it can't be on someone else's plot. It needs to be in between the plots or inside the fence, but outside the assigned graves."

"What is the difference between a graveyard and a cemetery?"

"A cemetery is essentially any burial ground; it doesn't have to be near, or associated with, a church. Commonly, they're burial grounds on private properties. A graveyard, on the other hand, is near a church and associated with the church. The reason it's important to find an old graveyard is because the church blesses the land. Over the years, the more blessing, the stronger the land is.”

“Thanks for all this information. I didn’t know there was a difference.”

“Do you need help? I can come over if you need me to.”

“No, I shouldn’t have any issues since it was all hypothetical.” Alice laughed.

“If you do ever need help or something becomes less hypothetical, please let me know.” Sage said goodbye and hung up.

Let’s do this.

Since Alice couldn’t call Alistair in the bathroom because of the wards, she placed the bowl on the dining room table. Opening the cabinet door, she pulled out the salt she’d bought earlier that day. Pouring a thin layer of salt on the bottom of the bowl, she reminded herself to make a note to buy more salt, since she had a feeling this would become a regular occurrence.

Taking a deep breath, she went into the closet where the dumbwaiter was. She pressed the button to call the dumbwaiter to the second floor. When it arrived, she opened the jewelry box inside the lift, not wanting to take any chances. Palming the watch, she closed the closet door but left the dumbwaiter door open in case she needed to return it quickly.

Leaving her bedroom, she saw Alistair watching her.

“Alistair, how are you today?”

“I’m good. Do I know you? I think I was pulled here.”

“We met a couple nights ago. I found a pocket watch, like you were asking for, but I don’t think it’s yours.” Alice sat at the table and slowly dropped the watch into the bowl. “Is this yours?”

Alistair moved closer to the table, his eyes fixated on the pocket watch. "I think so. Can I have it?"

"Unfortunately, no, you can't. I'm sorry." Alice covered the watch with salt, and a blinding light flashed from the bowl along with a popping sound.

When the spots dissolved from her vision, she glanced up and Alistair was still there. "Alistair? Do you know where you are?"

"No. I remember going for a drive, and then everything went black. Now, I'm here." Alistair scrutinized the area, as if he was unfamiliar with Alice or his surroundings.

"I don't know exactly what happened to you, but you died. You've been bound to a pocket watch by someone who, I think, wants you to find it for him."

"What kind of pocket watch?"

"It's a Thelemite pocket watch, similar to the ring you're wearing." Alice hadn't noticed Alistair was wearing a ring with the full Thelema symbol when he was there before.

"Put it away. Wherever you had it, put it away right now. Leave it in the salt." Alistair paced nervously, so Alice did as he'd asked.

She placed the bowl inside a plastic container so it wouldn't spill in the dumbwaiter. As she walked into her bedroom, she checked to make sure he didn't follow her.

Placing the container in the dumbwaiter, she closed the doors to it and the closet.

In the dining room, she saw Alistair sitting in a chair with his head in his hands.

"How are you sitting?"

"Ghosts can sit if they concentrate, or when they're highly emotional, their bodies can take on more of a solid form."

"Thanks. I'm new to this whole ghost thing."

"I can tell by the way you handled the pocket watch without care, like you did. How did you know I was bound?"

"I guessed, honestly. You only appeared once in a while, and you didn't remember much. I found an article about you being the Grand Marshal in a parade, and it physically hurt you to think about it. I also got a ghost book, read more into it, and thought maybe it could be the case."

"Book by Sage Wondyr?" Alistair's eyes teared up.

"How did you know?"

"I loved her before I got married and had my family. Trent, Sage, and I were the founders of a branch of Thelemism here in Florida. We had a falling out, and Sage left to open her witch shop. I stayed in the faith but left the building. The next thing I knew, Trent went crazy and started ranting and raving about ending the world. I tried to keep up with what Sage was doing, at least."

"I believe Trent may have brought you back to find the pocket watch so you could lead him to a box of some sort."

"Do you have the box? Is it safe?"

"If I had the box, it would be safe. To be honest, I'm not even sure what the box looks like to know if I have it or not."

"I understand. I don't feel under anyone else's control, but you never know with Trent. He has the money and power to influence people to do whatever he wants, apparently even after their deaths. Whatever you do, make sure anything you may have with the symbol of the Thelema on it is strongly protected. Trent and his goons will stop at nothing to pervert the faith."

"What does he want to do? I couldn't find anything which explains what could happen if he gets ahold of it."

"Trent is part of the Neo- Thelemism sect, which believes the end times are upon us. They want to unleash the gods of war and death to speed up the timeline for when Thelemites can take their rightful places next to the gods sooner rather than later."

"By using a box?"

"Allegedly, and who knows if any of this is even vaguely true, the gods were placed in an alternate dimension. Their immortality and power had caused issues on Earth, so the original Thelemites made a deal with them to allow them to go to this other dimension in exchange for magical abilities. The gods were tiring of Earth anyway, and there was so much infighting, they took it as an opportunity to spread out and expand their own personal fiefdoms in the alternate dimension."

"Why would the gods want to come back?"

"They probably don't. If the box is opened, they'll have the ability to, and if they wanted to, they could rain fire and have immense power over the world. Their power has only grown since they left."

"Why would they want to rain fire?"

"Because they're vengeful, and they love to create chaos. Obviously, that's assuming the stories are correct." Alistair shrugged. "I was in the faith because its principles rang true for me, but I'm peaceful, and definitely don't want to take part in something hurtful to others."

"So, they'd come back and destroy everything for fun? Why does this specific sect think they'd be accepted as gods for allowing the gods to come back instead of destroyed, like everyone else? Is it because they'd be given power and be able to restart the human race as a reward for releasing them?" Alice couldn't figure out why someone would do what Trent was proposing doing.

"I don't believe they've really thought it through. Honestly, it doesn't surprise me. The members who stayed after I left were all a little off. They're so entrenched in their belief that they're doing something they'll be rewarded for, they're willing to do almost anything. Speaking of which, what month is it?"

"It's the end of April. Why?" Alice was surprised by the quick change of topic but rolled with it.

"Trent always believed the best day to open the box and allow the gods back was on the Ides of May, which is coming up. For the ritual to take place, they need to have all the elements and time to prepare. If I'm not mistaken, he would need the box no later than May ninth to complete the process in time."

"What happens if he doesn't get the box and elements by then?"

"Everything becomes inert for the time being. Before I died, I saw Trent, and he was ranting about the watch and the box. I remember him talking about how if it isn't done soon, something will happen, and the elements will become inert, and their power will disappear forever. He must have brought me back to find the pocket watch."

"What's the importance of this watch?" Alice was forming a clearer picture of what was going on, and she just needed to outlast Trent.

"It helps find the box. The pocket watch was sent to me by one of the European chapters. It was my job to protect it and keep it away from the box."

"Why does it need to stay away from the box?" Alice was concerned about them being next to each other in the dumbwaiter.

"It's one of two things needed to open the box. From what I know, all three objects can be near each other. If a practitioner of the faith was to have all three, then they could open the box."

Breathing a sigh of relief, Alice heard her stomach growl, realizing she hadn't eaten recently.

"What is the second thing needed?"

"One of our rings." Alistar twisted the ring he wore. "It was supposed to connect us, not cause the end times."

"I'm sorry someone is twisting your faith. Is there anything else you know or want to let me know? I need to eat, and I think you're ready to cross over or whatever happens to ghosts when they're unbound or done with whatever their unfinished business is."

"One more thing if you can. I remember driving down a dirt road near Palm Coast. Could you have them check to see if my car or my body are somewhere along there? I'd like my wife and kids to have closure."

"I will, Alistair. Thanks for all your help."

"No, thank you, Alice. I'm sorry if I was rude to you earlier."

"You have nothing to be sorry for. None of this was your fault. Be at peace, Alistair."

Instead of Alistair fading away like Kyle did when he disappeared, his frame sparkled, and he vanished.

Alice called Officer Rivera to see if he was still on duty. Getting his voice mail, she left a message asking him to call her tomorrow afternoon. One 'issue' was out of the way, another live one to deal with later.

Chapter Eleven

Everything was quiet in the morning, so Alice checked her phone and saw Cynthia had texted her to let her know she would be there at around one.

Seeing it was after 11, Alice made herself breakfast and had an extra skip in her step. She felt good about what she'd done last night. Helping Alistair become unbound and free made her happy. He didn't deserve to be anyone's puppet, especially not Trent's.

Downstairs, she sat in the office drinking her tea and thinking about how she still hadn't found the book listing all the items sold, despite extensive cleaning, nor had she found anything about Kyle going to estate sales for new merchandise. She didn't believe he was lying, but it was strange. Did she have to buy many items, or would one thing start the cycle over?

She was still mulling it over when she heard the bell at the front door jingle.

Cynthia was coming in carrying two steaming coffee cups. Alice could smell the sweetness of green tea mixed with the scent of strong coffee.

"I didn't get you a coffee; I got you a black tea, but they use the same cups for everything." Cynthia smiled as she kicked the door closed and brought the drinks over to the counter.

"Thanks. You didn't have to bring me tea, but I appreciate it." Alice held up her mug.

"I figured with how much we need to accomplish over the next two days, it's for the best." They laughed as they sipped from their drinks.

"Is the goal still to knockout the stockroom today, see what time it is, and then try to head to the basement if there's time?"

"I think it's a realistic goal. I realize I haven't been down in the basement in a couple days, so I'm not quite sure how bad it is now. Before I forget, do you think you'll be comfortable opening and closing when I need to travel to buy more stuff?"

"Do you think you'll need to go soon?" Cynthia scanned the stockroom.

"Not necessarily. It was just something I was talking to my accountant about."

A little white lie never hurt anyone.

"Absolutely. We could even close for the day if the estate sales are close, so I could go with you. Have you thought about advertising that you're interested in buying estates?"

"No, I don't even have a website yet." Alice needed to add the website to her growing list of things to get done.

"Yes, you do. I made it for you the other day. It's plain right now, but we can add to it. I never asked, but do you plan to sell online?"

"Not yet, but eventually. I was thinking about doing it during the slow months, especially if it'll take up a lot of time. We don't want to stretch ourselves too thin."

"We should be fine, but you could also do a 'wish list' side where people send in what they're looking for."

"That's a good idea. Let's get to the stockroom, and you can show me the website during a break." Alice smiled as Cynthia jumped up and skipped to the back of the store.

Cynthia seemed to enjoy when people acknowledged the good things she did, and Alice had no problem encouraging her.

The remaining side of the stockroom took two hours to label and sort.

Alice was surprised how quickly they finished, but with two people and most of the stock already organized, it was easy. Taking a short break to drink their now cold drinks, they headed to the basement.

It was significantly fuller than when Alice had last visited. While good for her income, it was terrible for her organization.

"How do you want to tackle this?" Cynthia moved a box of hood ornaments from classic cars to the side so they could walk in deeper.

"Let's start near the stairs and work our way back."

A short time later, Alice thought she heard the jingle of the bell on the front door.

"Did you hear something?"

"No, all this dust is making the blood rush through my ears thanks to my sinuses, and I'm sneezing so much. What did you hear?"

"I thought I heard the jingle of the bell. Let me go upstairs really quick and make sure no one came into the store."

Alice took the stairs two at a time. Opening the door to the first floor, she didn't immediately see anything unusual.

"Hello?" she called out to what she hoped was an empty storefront. Not seeing or hearing anything, as she went to return to the basement, she saw a flash of someone moving. Wishing she had a weapon, she went to the front door, looking for anything she could swing at an attacker. Grabbing a tennis racket older than she was, she tiptoed through the building.

Alice noticed someone bent over a box in the sports section. She swung the racket for all she was worth, but her swing was stopped in midair on its descent.

A skeleton hand held the racket.

She let go in fear and heard a gravelly voice come from behind her.

"No need for violence."

She followed the blue cloak from the hand to the rest of the body and realized the cloak covered everything, head to toe.

"Who are you? Why are you in my store?"

"Apologies. My friend was assigned a job in your store, which will occur in about 15 minutes, and we haven't visited since the new owner took possession. We just wanted to take a look around and see what they've done with the place."

"Sorry, but we're closed today, and I don't know what kind of job your friend could possibly have since I don't remember hiring anyone other than Cynthia."

"Oh dear, my mistake. We haven't properly introduced ourselves. Dahlia, stop digging around in the photo bin and come introduce yourself like a civilized person."

Alice stepped to the side so she could see both intruders in front of her.

The cloaked figure was taller than Alice, probably barely under six feet.

The other was short, five two at the most. Alice realized the woman was the same person she'd run into on the street the day the store opened. She was about Alice's age, with light hair and blue eyes. She'd thought she'd seen the blue cloak somewhere before as well.

"Hi, I'm Dahlia. Can you please leave so I can do my job in – now 11 minutes?"

"I don't know who you are, but you're not coming into my store and telling me to leave."

"Oh, honey. Bless your heart. You think you have any control over me?" The short one laughed with her hands over her heart.

"Now Dahlia, this is no way to treat your new neighbor," the figure scolded.

"It doesn't matter. She'll be gone soon, anyway. The newcomers always are. For some reason, your kind can't seem to handle the heat – or this building." The woman crossed her arms over her chest as she looked Alice up and down.

"I bought it right after Kyle died. Didn't I?"

Dahlia laughed. "Gosh no, why do you think you paid so little for it? There were at least five owners between Kyle's death and you buying it."

"But I bought it from Kyle's family." Alice was confused and didn't like it.

"You did, but the previous 'owners' left so fast Kyle's estate was forced to take it back each time. They left before the ink was dry, so to speak. Anyway, none of that's important since you'll be gone within a month."

"You don't know me. You have no idea what I can and cannot handle. Leave before I call the police."

Before the woman could argue, Alice heard Cynthia yelling for her. She wanted to yell back and tell her it was too dangerous, but Cynthia ran upstairs from the basement before she could. She stopped short, about ten feet from Dahlia and the stranger.

"Cynthia, it's alright. I don't think they're here to hurt us."

Cynthia narrowed her eyes at the stranger before looking at the woman with surprise and recognition. "Dahlia?"

"Yes, who are you?"

"You don't remember me? I haven't seen you in years."

"Before we get too deep into this, how do you know her, Cynthia?" Alice wanted them to leave, and it sounded more like a family reunion.

"She's my uncle's ex-wife." Cynthia stayed where she was but continued to glance back and forth between them.

"Great, now that we know each other's names and relationships, can you two please leave?"

"I found something," Cynthia said as Kyle popped up behind her.

"What did you find?" Alice stepped closer to Cynthia.

"Not now. We have an unwanted visitor about to come through the window," Kyle announced, and Cynthia whipped around.

"Who are you, and where did you come from?" Cynthia jumped away from Kyle, almost bumping into Alice.

"Who's coming, Kyle?" Alice tried to keep Cynthia from running. It took a minute to click that Cynthia had seen Kyle.

"It's the reason Dahlia's here. I don't know why David's here, though." Kyle pointed at the tall cloaked stranger.

"I may have to help Dahlia. Cynthia and Alice, I think you should both go back downstairs please, or upstairs, either way. Just don't stay here." David faced Cynthia.

"No. This is my business, and I'm staying."

"Suit yourself. Cynthia?"

"Nope. I'm not going anywhere. I want answers. Now." Cynthia intertwined her arm with Alice's. They took a simultaneous step back toward the counter when the front window shattered, and Trent burst through.

"Alice, I've come for what you owe me. I know you have it. I could feel it last night."

"Trent? Why didn't you use the damn door? It's unlocked."

Trent's eyes were wild, and Alice took a step back.

"I STILL have no clue what you're talking about. But you *are* breaking and entering, so you need to leave right now." Alice's phone rang with a call from Officer Rivera. She stayed calm as she answered, "Good afternoon, Officer Rivera. Thank you for returning my call."

"Anytime. Is this a good time?"

"It's actually a great time. Someone's breaking into my shop while Cynthia and I are here working. Would it be possible for you to come get Trent Benson?"

"Trent broke into your shop? Are you and Cynthia alright?"

"We're fine, but there's a lot of damage to the front window from where he came through it. I worry because the lights are dim, and someone could trip and cut themselves on the glass or impale themselves on something he knocked over."

"You and Cynthia need to get out of there right now. I'll be there in less than 20 minutes."

"Thank you." Alice hung up and stared at Trent.

"What do you think your precious officer can do? I have all the power. Now, give me the box."

"Trent, I don't think this is a good idea. You need to leave while you still can," the stranger Kyle had referred to as David said.

"David, what a pleasant surprise. Is your little puppy dog around as well?" Trent tittered.

"Scorch is at home."

"I don't mean your actual dog, you fool. I mean the reaper who follows you around like a puppy."

"You mean me?" Dahlia stood scowling, pointing a corn-cob pipe at Trent.

"Yes. I assume you're here because one of these bitches over there is going to die?" Trent taunted Dahlia while staring at Alice and Cynthia.

"Not at all. They'll be fine. You, on the other hand, are about" — she pulled out her phone and looked at the time — "90 seconds from dying."

"Impossible. The box and pocket watch are coming with me, and I will be a god." Trent dug through boxes, throwing items everywhere.

"Now I'm going to have to clean that up, Trent, just leave." Alice's patience was wearing thin.

"70 seconds." Dahlia's pipe morphed into a large scythe.

Alice couldn't believe what she was seeing.

"Do you see what I see?" Alice whispered to Cynthia.

"A scythe being wielded by my former aunt? Yup. Are we going crazy?" Cynthia questioned Alice.

"Who knows anymore? This building is probably full of lead or mold or something." Alice hadn't the faintest idea. This was so far out of her wheelhouse; it was completely insane.

Trent sauntered over to Alice while Dahlia was still counting down the minutes.

"Stop it. I'm not dying." Trent stepped over a basket holding the religious artifacts the techs had found when they had searched for his items.

David stepped closer to Trent, causing him to misjudge where his foot would land.

"Five." Dahlia called out.

Trent stepped down onto a frisbee, causing his foot to slide forward.

Unable to grab onto anything, Alice watched in slow motion as he fell backwards onto the sword from the Archangel Michael paperweight she had seen earlier.

A faint image of him rose above his body, and Dahlia quickly swiped through it with her scythe.

The scattered pieces floated briefly, and Alice saw black sparkles before it completely vanished.

"Um, what just happened?"

"We don't have time for that right now. Your 'friend' the cop will be here any minute. I wasn't here, and you never saw me." Dahlia touched the scythe, and it turned back into a cob pipe. She strolled out the front door without a care in the world and turned left, the door slamming behind her.

David came up to Alice and Cynthia. "I'll be back after Officer Rivera leaves. Don't go anywhere, Alice. We need to have a conversation when this is all over. Cynthia, you can go if the officer says you can."

Alice nodded at the deep voice, and between blinks, he was gone.

"Are you okay, Alice?" She heard Officer Rivera's voice from outside the broken window.

"Yeah, let me get the door. You need to call an ambulance, or the morgue, or whoever you call in this situation. Cynthia will get the lights." She glanced back at Cynthia, who was already moving toward the switch.

"Are you injured?" He looked her over when she opened the door.

"No, but Trent Benson is." She motioned toward the bleeding body of Trent.

Rivera rushed to his side and checked his pulse.

"I need to call this in. You and Cynthia will need to give your statements."

"We aren't going anywhere." Alice and Cynthia sat in chairs near the register as the ambulance came and retrieved Trent's body after techs took pictures.

"This is Officer Brant. She'll be taking Cynthia's statement, and I can take yours."

Alice nodded at Cynthia before walking away.

"Can you tell me what happened?"

"Cynthia and I were down in the basement organizing. We heard a noise, so we came up. I thought it was a rock or brick at first, but I saw Trent climbing through the window demanding I give him what was his."

"What happened next?"

"I grabbed a tennis racket and stood my ground when he stepped over the basket and onto the frisbee. When his foot hit the frisbee, it slid out from under him, and he fell backwards onto the paperweight. I dropped the racket and went to check to see if he was still alive, but there was so much blood, and I didn't want to get too close."

"What did you call me about earlier? Was it about Trent?"

"No. Actually, I'd overheard someone talking about Alistair Sinclair. They'd said he used to go for drives down a dirt road near Palm Coast when he needed to think, and you'd mentioned he was missing, so I thought I'd mention it in case he's out there somewhere."

"Thanks, I'll definitely check it out tomorrow. Office Brant is finished as well, so you and Cynthia can go. To discourage thieves or wild animals, I'd suggest putting a piece of plywood over the window until you can get it fixed."

"I will. Thank you, Officer Rivera." Alice shook his hand before leaning back in her chair.

Cynthia came over and sat next to her. "What do we do now?"

"Now we wait. They'll leave, David will be back, and I need to go get plywood for the window."

"Don't worry about the plywood. I'll have Jake bring some over. We still have some leftover from last hurricane season."

"Cynthia, if he's off work, you can go. Don't worry about me."

"It's okay. I already called him. He's on his way."

"Thanks. Do you still want to work here? I know your first week has been crazy."

"Absolutely. This is the most fun I've had in a long time. I have a question, though."

"Yes?"

"Who was the guy who popped up behind me talking about Trent before he broke through the window?"

"So, you *did* see him?"

"And heard him. Did he come through the side door or in with Aunt Dahlia and the guy in the cloak?"

Before Alice could respond, she heard a man's voice call for Cynthia.

"I think Jake's here," Alice said as Cynthia saw him walk through the door.

"Hi, you must be Alice." Jake held out his hand to Cynthia.

"I am. Thank you for bringing over the plywood. You didn't have to. How much do I owe you?"

"It was left over and taking up space in the garage from last hurricane season, so don't worry about it. Are you okay, Cynthia?" Jake hugged Cynthia.

Alice heard her muffled yes.

"I'm sorry all this happened."

"You couldn't have predicted a crazy man would break in. With the way Cynthia talks about you, I'm sure you could've protected you both."

Alice smiled. "I'd like to think so. If you're ready to leave, I can put up the wood myself."

"I'll take care of it. Cynthia, please stay in here while I do."

Cynthia smiled before sitting back down.

"The man?"

"You've been through a lot today. Maybe we should talk about it tomorrow." Alice didn't know how to tell Cynthia she'd seen and heard a ghost.

"It wasn't a living man, was it?"

"Why do you ask?"

"It was like I could almost see through him, but not quite. Like he was there, but not at the same time."

"Yes, he's a ghost."

"How long have you been able to see him?"

"Pretty much since I bought the property. Before you ask, no, I'd never seen a ghost before I moved here."

"Who is it?"

"It's the former owner, Kyle Morgan. You're taking all this much better than I did. I thought I had a tumor or something."

Cynthia laughed without humor. "My family has talked about ancestors who could see ghosts. I didn't know if I ever would. In the past, there were times I thought I'd seen something out of the corner of my eye, but never as clear as he was."

"Listen, if this is all too much, you don't have to keep working here. I'll still pay you for the six months like we agreed."

Cynthia reached over and grabbed Alice's hands. "Absolutely not. Believe it or not, I feel like I have more purpose and drive now than I ever did sitting behind a desk. I can create things, like the flyer and your website. I can move around freely, and I'm enjoying myself."

"If you're sure. But if it ever gets to a point where it's too much, you can leave."

"I'm already looking at houses. You aren't getting rid of me so easily." This time, Cynthia's laugh reached her eyes.

Alice joined in as they listened to the murmur of the police and Jake's hammering. Soon, the police left, leaving the pool of blood on the floor.

Cynthia worked on cleaning it up when Jake came inside saying he'd finished.

Alice told Cynthia to leave it and she would finish cleaning herself.

After Cynthia told Alice she would be there at around one the next day, they left, Jake's arm slung across Cynthia's shoulders.

Alice watched them leave and felt sad for a minute.

Right before they left the store, Cynthia turned around. "I almost forgot. I found a random birth certificate. It was odd, so I wanted to show you. I left it under the register."

"Thanks." Alice waved at them.

As she cleaned, she felt a presence and gave the room a once-over.

David was standing there near a cabinet of framed photos. At least, she assumed it was him, considering whoever it wore the same blue cloak.

"Can I help you, or do you plan on watching me clean without offering to help?"

"Sorry, I didn't mean to frighten you."

"You grabbed me earlier with your bone hands, and you disappeared in front of me. I assume you're the 'Death' Kyle told me about?"

"How much has he told you?"

"Enough to know you used him as a secure location for things. I'm guessing you're also who's responsible for the Thelema items everyone seems to want."

"Guilty, but I didn't think it would come to this."

"Thanks. What did you think it would come to, then? I'd give it to them without a fuss? I wouldn't care someone tried to break in, and I was getting strange calls? Not hear ghosts?"

"I knew you'd hear ghosts."

"What?"

"Anyway, can I have the things?"

"No, because I don't know which 'things' you're referring to. Everyone seems to want me to miraculously know what they're looking for. You can answer what you meant about me hearing ghosts any time now."

"Yeah, about the ghosts. You might want to look at the birth certificate Cynthia found, but after you give me the things, please."

"Nuh uh. You will answer me." Alice stood with her hands on her hips.

"You see, you come from a line of people who can see ghosts."

"No, my parents are ordinary people from Oregon. Nothing special about them other than my mom could grow tomatoes without any issues."

It looked like Death was trying to avoid the question, which interested Alice. This was supposedly an immortal being, and yet she knew he was lying.

"How about we talk about this later? I need the items, and I promise I'll come back so we can talk about it."

"No, you sound like a used car salesman. Why do you think I'll give you what you want? Because you told me to? No, you'll answer my questions, and then I'll decide if I'm going to give them to you. They're safe where they are right now."

Alice heard him sigh before he sat in the chair Cynthia had sat in. In his hand was a single piece of paper he handed to Alice. "Here, this is your original birth certificate."

It was a Florida birth certificate, but instead of her parent's names, there was another mother with no father listed.

"She was 17 and gave you up for adoption. Your parents adopted you when you were a day old."

"So, who's my father?"

"I'm not all knowing."

Alice glared at him.

"Seriously, I don't know. I know your birth mother had the sight, and it's genetic, so you must have gotten it from her."

"You knew my birth mother?"

"I was there when she died, but I didn't know her."

"Oh. I guess that makes it all better than, right? You swoop in, change my entire life, tell me the only parents I've ever known aren't my biological parents. I guess I should be thanking you. What are you going to do with these things you need? Are you going to tell me what they are? I want answers, and I won't give you anything until you tell me." Alice couldn't focus on finding out more about her birth mother right now. Not when Death was sitting next to her.

"It's the two items from the Thelema religion you have, the box and the watch. The ring, I'll acquire later. I know you have both, but I don't know where. There's an acquaintance of mine who's going to be visiting their creator."

"So, you truly aren't all knowing." Alice smirked. "So, it's true? Does the box hold passage for the Gods?"

"No, it holds the souls of monsters, and I mean human monsters."

"Why was it created, then?"

"It's a long boring story you don't need to know, but the one responsible for creating it is working with others to release the souls in a matter which keeps them from causing harm."

"Yeah, I'm sure that's what'll happen."

Death looked up at Alice, and his two red eyes pierced the dark. They were similar but slightly different from the eyes watching over her a previous night.

"Let's hope you're wrong." Death stood.

"I'll grab them. You can stay here." Alice's brain was still trying to decide if she should return them to him, but she knew deep down she was going to, and it was the right thing to do.

Opening the dumbwaiter, she called it down to her. When it arrived, she pulled out the bowl with the pocket watch, the puzzle box, and the jewelry box.

Death was right behind her with his boney hands reaching for the items.

"I had to unbind a spirit, so the watch is in the bowl, but you can keep it."

"Thanks, I guess. I don't need the jewelry box. It has no actual connection to the pocket watch or the puzzle box."

"Seriously? You're saying I was protecting a useless jewelry box?"

"It was a place to put the pocket watch. Anyway, thank you for this. I'll be going."

"Death, can I ask you something before you leave?"

"Please call me David. I hate being called by my title all the time."

"Sorry, David, did you meet my husband when he died?"

"No, I only deal with souls fighting to stay around. The reaper who released his soul from his body said he went quickly."

"Thank you." Alice didn't know if she was happy or sad he hadn't tried to stay around.

"It's the preferred way. It can get messy otherwise." David turned to leave.

"Thank you. Will I see you again?"

"I'm sure you will." One second he was there and the next he wasn't.

Alice went over to the counter and picked up the birth certificate.

A problem for another day.

Alice trudged upstairs. In her kitchen, she saw a cup of tea was waiting for her, still steaming. Smiling, she looked up at the ceiling. "Thank you."

Picking up the tea, she went to her bedroom and changed for bed. She only drank half the tea before she fell asleep.

Love, you did a good thing today. Nathan appeared in Alice's dream.

It doesn't feel like it.

You helped someone, and you'll continue to help people. Lean on those who care about you. Make friends with Dahlia. She'll help you.

Who? The grouchy woman who calls herself a reaper?

Yes. You'll find you need her.

Like I need a thorn in my hand.

Just trust me. I love you.

I love you too, Alice said as Nathan faded away, and Alice slipped into a deeper sleep.

Kyle stood next to her bed as she slept. "This is only the beginning, Alice. We have a long way to go before it's over."

He picked up the cup and took it into the kitchen.

About the Author

F.L. Journey is the pen name for two authors who have come together to write in a variety of genres they enjoy. Look for more short stories and novels in the future from them.

Follow us on Facebook, Goodreads, and Amazon.

Facebook: https://www.facebook.com/FLJourney
Amazon: https://amzn.to/2S3cCbi
Goodreads: https://bit.ly/30bl6By

Acknowledgements

We would like to thank Terry Journey for alpha reading, Melanie Marsh for Editing, and Crystal and Elise for their great PA work. Without you four this book wouldn't have happened.

Books by F.L Journey

Ancient Resurgence Series
Ancient Resurgence – Daniel's Story
Ancient Resurgence

Cerberus Brothers
Cobalt Warrior
Crimson Scholar
Jade Commander

Matching Galaxies
Princess and the Pirate

Once Upon a Midlife
Forgotten Echoes
Cursed Mirror – (Coming Fall 2025)

Anthologies
NIWA Illusions – Death Awaits
Little Witches - Growing up Twin Witch
Dark Descent: Whispers from Beyond – Night Terrors

Books by Flo Journey

PNW Syndicates
Carlina
Beatrice (Coming late 2025)

Anthologies
Holiday Anthology (Coming November 2025)
Violence and Virtues (Coming February 2026)
Sins and Seduction Vol 1 (Coming October 2026)

www.ingramcontent.com/pod-product-compliance
Lightning Source LLC
Chambersburg PA
CBHW020803310726
48969CB00002B/670